A NECKLACE OF WORDS

A Necklace of Words

Stories by Mexican Women

Edited By
Marjorie Agosín
&
Nancy Abraham Hall

White Pine Press • Fredonia, New York

Publication of this book was made possible, in part, by grants from the National Endowment for the Arts, the New York State Council on the Arts, and the Fideicomiso Para La Cultura Mexico-USA and its three sponsors, Fundación Cultural Bancomer, The Rockefeller Foundation, and the Fondo Nacional para la Cultura y las Artes.

Acknowledgments:
Excerpt from *The Nine Guardians* by Rosario Castellanos translated by Irene Nicholson. English translation copyright Faber and Faber Ltd., 1959. Reprinted by arrangement with Readers International, Inc.

Excerpt from *Recollections of Things to Come* by Elena Garro, translated by Ruth L. C. Simms, Copyright ©1969. By permission of the University of Texas Press.

Cover painting by Heteo Perez

Book design by Elaine LaMattina

Manufactured in the United States of America

10 9 8 7 6 5 4 3 2 1

ISBN 1-877727-73-3

Published by
White Pine Press, 10 Village Square, Fredonia, New York 14063

To Angelina Muñiz Huberman,
who showed me a secret threshold of words and beauty,
and to all the Mexican women writers
of the past, the present, and the future.
—M.A.

For my teacher Joaquina Navarro.
—N.A.H.

CONTENTS

INTRODUCTION

MARJORIE AGOSÍN
&
NANCY ABRAHAM HALL

Mexico, imagined and imaginary, opposite and vulnerable. Mexico extends itself before the eyes of outsiders and insiders as a place of honor and unexpected colors: jade green, mallow, cobalt blue. Mexico is a territory where hands exercise the wise artistry of clay, paper flowers, candy skulls–the skulls of death. Writers and artists from other cultures have yearned to understand a Mexico which interweaves Pre-Hispanic traditions with a modernity unique to the Western World. As foreigners in this country of marvels, exuberance and austerity André Breton, Graham Greene, Tina Modotti, D.H. Lawrence, Katherine Anne Porter, Edward Weston, Harriet Doerr, and so many others have viewed what Mexico had to offer–an autocthonous, syncretic culture forged of eternal masks and magic herbs, disparate chronologies and transcendent myths–through lenses crafted beyond the border. Conversely, Frida Kahlo and Diego Rivera inserted the art of Europe into that of Mexico by focusing on the concept of a hybrid and transparent nation, at once sophisticated and innocent, steeped in its own violence. As artists, they invented themselves, but they also invented Mexico.

Within the realm of the Latin American imagination Mexico

has always been a space in which fables and truths are created, a country of ancient gods and valiant kings, ruthless conquerors and zealous missionaries, brilliant humanists and tireless warriors, incomparable artists, poets and storytellers. The names Quetzalcóatl, Cuauhtémoc, Hernán Cortés, La Malinche, Bernal Díaz del Castillo, Fray Bartolomé de las Casas, Sor Juana Inés de la Cruz, Benito Juárez, Emiliano Zapata, Pancho Villa, Alfonso Reyes, Rufino Tamayo, Juan Rulfo, Rosario Castellanos, Octavio Paz, Elena Poniatowska and Carlos Fuentes have been indelibly etched in the collective mind and soul of the entire Spanish-speaking world. And yet these names only begin to define what it means to be Mexican, to belong to one of the most dynamic, multifaceted, and astonishing cultures of the American continent.

Across the centuries, the women of Mexico have made important contributions to the cultural life of the nation. As archetypes they play essential roles in foundational stories. None more revered and reviled than La Malinche (also known as Malintzin Tenepal and Doña Marina) mother of the mestizo people, whose own dual nature suggests that of the country's history, a record which depends above all on who tells it and who remembers it. None more beloved than the Virgin of Guadalupe, the dark-skinned Madonna who appears to barefoot Juan Diego on the Tepeyac mountainside, not far from the ancient devotional center of the mother-goddess Tonantzin. None more tragic than La Llorona, wailing for the babies she drowned when driven mad by her husband's infidelity, or more celebrated than Adelita, riding alongside troops determined to unseat the usurper Victoriano Huerta during the Mexican Revolution.

As anonymous artisans, the women of Mexico have sustained

a very rich and awe-inspiring tradition of craftmanship that is central to the nation's cultural identity. In remote towns and villages generations of women potters, weavers, woodcarvers and embroiderers create vessels, garments and other useful objects of amazing beauty which transcend domestic purposes. Born of women's everyday experience and necessity, these humble crafts have passed into the public sphere of aesthetic accomplishment, and are today displayed in museums and sought by collectors around the world

Women writers, critics, and visual artists have also moved, in increasing numbers, and despite the still pervasive machismo of Mexico's intellectual and artistic circles, to the central spaces of cultural life. It is there that Sor Juana Inés de la Cruz, the nun who chose learning, is now accompanied by, among others: Frida Kahlo, the painter who depicts her own physical and emotional anguish; Rosario Castellanos, the diplomat who gives a voice to the indigenous people of Chiapas; Leonora Carrington, the British-born creator of mythical and dream-like fantasies on canvas; Amalia Hernández, the choreographer who founded and inspires the world-renowned Ballet Folklórico; Elena Poniatowska, the descendant of Polish aristocrats who bears witness to the massacre at Tlatelolco; Graciela Iturbide, the photographer who honors the spirit of Mexico's indigenous women; and Marta Palau, the multimedia artist whose tapestries, sculptures, and acrylics tap the rich vein of shared human memory. These women have gained entry into a canonical history that simultaneously embraces and shuns their work. By creating alternatives to the usual brand of heroism, they have forged their own stories, and found thoroughly original ways to participate in the national culture. It is impossible to consider Mexican baroque poetry without Sor Juana, indigenism without Castellanos, and contemporary Mexican history without Poniatowska.

The present anthology, the first of its kind in the United States, gathers the voices of noteworthy Mexican women writers of the twentieth century in English translation. While one of the selections first appeared sixty years ago, and another in 1957, the majority are by authors who began to write and publish in the sixties, when an emergent middle class supported an unprecedented boom in Mexican letters. Joining women from across Latin America, these authors have built a sense of solidarity across national boundaries, not only as women who write, but as women who publish to create a voice and to further public discourse. This book presents selections in prose by a variety of women writers who offer unique perspectives on Mexican history, society, and cultural values. Through their use of language, their lyricism, their eroticism, the reader discovers the intangible and real Mexico.

* * *

The anthology begins with a trio of writers whose focus is Mexican history. The opening selection, from *Cartucho* (1940) is by the lone woman writer of the immediate post-Revolutionary period: Nelly Campobello. A journalist by trade, and ardent admirer of Francisco Villa, Campobello published two novels and several short stories based on memories of her childhood in the war-ravaged northern state of Durango. In these semi-autobiographical and profoundly historical vignettes, daily horrors of the Revolution are narrated by the voice of a young and curiously dispassionate child. Campobello's texts are often predictable, most notably in their loving idealization of a mother by her young daughter and the author's uncritical view of Pancho Villa; yet their remarkable strangeness lies in several detailed descriptions of the bloody, bullet-riddled, sometimes horribly mutilated bodies of the war's victims as seen through unblinking eyes: "Our streets would be left strewn with those strong young bodies, scattered on the ground on top of the hems their mamas had stitched into their shirts. What use were they? Why did they make them? How many pounds of flesh would they come to in total? How many eyes and thoughts?"

While Campobello uses a child's persepective to evoke a specific time and place in Mexico's history, novelist Elena Garro employs a collective narrator, the small rural town of Ixtepec, to write about the Cristero rebellion of the twenties. *Recuerdos del porvenir* (Recollections of Things to Come, 1963), Garro's masterpiece, and a structural precursor of García Márquez' *One Hundred Years of Solitude*, depicts a violent world in which love is impossible to attain. In the excerpt included in this anthology, several narrowminded townspeople mingle with the government soldiers and officers who occupy Ixtepec under the ruthless command of General Francisco Rosas. As he closes churches and imprisons his detractors, Rosas becomes increasingly jealous and possessive of his aloof and strangely impassive mistress, Julia, whose incomparable beauty holds the town transfixed. Inaccessible and alienated in her pale pink dress and vanilla-scented perfume, Julia personifies the anemic state of Ixtepec's collective soul. Garro makes clear her cynicism concerning the promise of the Revolution, as she depicts the lives of reactionary Mexicans who yearn for liberation by the *zap-*

atistas, yet despise and oppress one another as well as the Indian community of the area.

If Nelly Campobello and Elena Garro set their fiction in the turbulent early decades of the twentieth century, essayist and screenwriter Inés Arredondo travels further back in time to offer a new interpretation of a central historical figure: La Malinche. Following the publication of her award-winning short story collection *Río subterráneo* (Subterranean River), Arredondo wrote a children's book designed to counter the misogynistic historicism that has viewed Cortes' interpreter, guide, and mistress as betrayer, willing victim of rape, slut. In *Historia verdadera de una princesa* (The True Story of a Princess, 1984) the emphasis is on La Malinche's gifts as a linguist and diplomat, developed as she silently watches her beloved father, the King, before his untimely death. The princess' destiny—her role as mother of the mestizo people through her union with Cortés—is fulfilled thanks to the political machinations of a cruel stepmother, who sells the girl into slavery, and eventual contact with the conquistador. Never a traitor, but rather the victim of betrayal herself, Arredondo's Malinche forgives her stepmother in the end, making reconciliation the trademark of a new world order in which conqueror and vanquished live in peace and harmony.

The historical fact of *mestizaje,* that is, the mixing of the Indian and white races, and the essential impact of surviving indigenous cultures on every aspect of the Mexican soul and society is the central concern of the four selections included in the second part of this anthology. In "Regarding My Mestiza Self" from *Memorias de un mestizaje* (1994), Marcela Guijosa echoes Arredondo's yearning for what could have been: a process of racial crossbreeding characterized by equality, mutual respect and understanding, a careful forging of a dignified and peaceful future for all peoples of mixed race. Guijosa eloquently expresses the disorientation, pain and deep sense of loss she shares with other contemporary, urban, and biracial Mexican woman who wish to reconcile two such disparate heritages within their own hearts and minds.

A wish to explore, understand, and honor the indigenous roots and reality of Mexican culture informs the next three selections as well. In "Annunciation," the final chapter from *Isomorfismos* (1991), novelist, essayist, and short-story writer Esther Seligson weaves a dream-like tale of a young man accompanied by the voice of his Aztec grandfather and by ancient rituals and signs in a journey across the Mexican landscape. The odyssey leads to a surrender of the individual to the spirit, to the beloved, to the sea. At the author's request, we have provided a glossary of the Nahuatl words which appear in the chapter, so that English-speaking readers will not be denied the unique sounds, meanings, and textures they bring to this remarkable piece.

The profound messages that resonate in a single word, in a single name, also play an important role in the lyrical and sensual text by Sara Sefchovich. The narrator evokes layer upon layer of the Mexican landscape, its peaks and valleys, cities and villages, lakes, basins, rivers, ponds, streams, plants and animals, through a recitation of their spellbinding names, sometimes indigenous, sometimes Spanish, names that define the genealogy of a nation and a people. Excerpted from the novel *Demasiado amor* (Too Much Love, 1982), these passages and their narrator actually become Mexico, a land in search of origins, identity, knowledge of ancestors and self.

Like Seligson, Sefchovich, and de Anhalt, her friends and contemporaries with whom she shares Jewish ancestry, Margo Glantz is interested in life journeys, the messages in names, and the palpable survival of the past in the present. Professor, critic, poet, former cultural attaché to the Mexican government in London, she is the author of more than twenty-five books, ranging from a quirky "dietetic" novel to a profound memoir written primarily in the voice of her Russian Ukraine grandfather, Jacobo Glantz, a first-generation Mexican Jew. In *Síndrome de naufragios* (Shipwreck Syndrome, 1984), Glantz achieves a dazzling strangeness through more than forty meditations/stories about famous travelers, such as Noah, Columbus, Sinbad, Magellan, and Marco Polo who, this time around, are accompanied by an incredible cast of characters including Virginia Woolf, Cassandra, Abelard and Eloise, and the Marx Brothers, to name only a few. From this collection comes "Coatlicue Swept," in which the fierce Aztec mother goddess performs housework, her children wage bloody civil war, tiny automobiles dutifully stop at traffic lights within the main temple, and heaven and earth spring from the belly of a disemboweled Assyrian goddess. Glantz combines ancient myths with familiar objects to create a totally original pastiche in defiance of predictable categories of time, space, and cultural history. Primal violence coexist with mundane routine, as the old and the new, the mythic and the everyday are tangled in ways uniquely Mexican, but also universal, human.

We close the section with an excerpt from the classic novel *Balún Canán* (The Nine Guardians, 1957) by the incomparable Rosario Castellanos who held numerous teaching and diplomatic posts, and died while serving as Mexico's ambassador to

Israel. As a writer Castellanos cultivated every available genre: poetry, drama, literary criticism, essay, short story, novel. Balún Canán is Comitán, a small colonial center in the southern state of Chiapas much like the town in which Castellanos spent her relatively privileged childhood. The chapter we have selected brings into sharp focus the gaping chasm separating the Indian and white worlds of the author's youth, a chasm that persists virtually unchanged to the present day. Early in the novel the young narrator suffers a loss of innocence when she comes to a painful realization: her father, lounging in his hammock, may speak the language of the Indians who come to work his fields, but he is ignorant of, or indifferent to, the vengeful spirits that literally tear the flesh of the beloved nanny who tends to his children with kindness and love. Repelled by her father's role as white master, the narrator willfully breaks into a circle of Indians sipping coffee around the kitchen hearth, a circle which she knows is drawing tighter and is about to close, leaving her forever on the outside.

The authors whose work we include in the third section of this anthology are also concerned with closed-off spaces. However, these are spaces that confine, spaces from which characters yearn to escape: the small prisons of custom and tradition that dictate conformity, the death house of civil war that forces exiles to a new land, the abyss of economic disadvantage that keeps people hungry and destroys the natural environment.

We begin with Silvia Molina's "Sunday" from *Un hombre cerca* (A Man Nearby, 1992), about a woman who quietly breaks society's rules by taking responsibility for her own happiness. When she finds herself alone in a hotel room by the sea, however, she is overcome by tender memories of the ritual-filled

Sundays of her girlhood: leisurely strolls with her parents through Alameda Park, sugary cotton candy, taxi rides to grandmother's house for the afternoon meal, and the names and colors of all the flowers that grew in her grandfather's garden. As an adult, the narrator has rejected the traditional path of marriage, children, and family dinners, yet despite her independence, she longs for a man around the house, a special companion with whom to share her Sundays.

Family rituals are also the concern of Mónica Lavín, who creates a simple yet moving portrait of four generations of mothers and daughters in "Nicolasa and the Lacework," from the collection of the same name, *Nicolasa y los encajes* (1991). The story opens in pre-Civil War Spain, where a spirited young girl yearns to be free of the old-fashioned obligation of lace-making. The delicate border she creates that day for a pillowcase will bind her daughter and granddaughters across oceans and years, through war and exile, to settlement in a new land, where the ancestral voices of European immigrants meld with and enrich the hybrid culture that is contemporary Mexico.

Flight from fascist Spain is also a key element in Angeles Mastretta's "White Lies," an originally untitled piece from *Mujeres de ojos grandes* (Women with Big Eyes, 1990). Following the success of her best selling novel *Arráncame la vida* (Mexican Bolero, 1986), Mastretta turned her attention to a gallery of masterful stories about a series of aunts, each more vividly rendered than the next. Among them is Aunt Charo, a consummate gossip who knows everything that goes on "beneath all the skirts and pants" in Puebla. Charo's quick, merciless tongue is always able "to get to the core of any intrigue, to discover the divine oversight behind a person's ugliness, or to

latch onto the verbal miscue that would betray the candid soul."
But when a rumor not of her making suggests that the new
priest in town is in fact a godless Republican who has fled
Franco's Spain, Aunt Charo surprises even herself by sowing the
seeds of tolerance in her otherwise conservative and close-mind-
ed corner of the world.

The stories we have chosen by Molina, Lavín, and Mastretta
focus on well-to-do women characters whose challenges are
other than economic. Noted journalist Cristina Pacheco, however, writes of the urban poor who make up a disproportionate
percentage of the country's population. In the title story from
Sopita de fideo (Noodle Soup, 1989), a nighttime accident on a
Mexico City subway car conveys a heartbreaking truth: an adolescent girl charged with delivering a meager but lovingly prepared meal to her laborer father will be severely punished for her
failure to carry out the errand. Pacheco makes clear that basic
survival in a capital plagued by ever-worsening social and economic conditions (inadequate housing, overpopulation, under
and unemployment) comes down to a matter of luck, as many
hard-working, heroic families sink further and further into
despair.

Basic survival is an issue not only for vast numbers of
Mexico's people, but for the country's wild life and environment
as well. In "The Turtle," novelist and short-story writer Brianda
Domecq focuses on the activity of poachers who comb moonlit
beaches in search of female turtles and their nests. For Domecq,
the turtle is a creature in touch with "the secret fibers of ancestral memory," and this lyrical portrait of one particular creature's underwater life is dominated by references to the "voice of
the sea and the colors of the air, the coming and going of mil-

lions of years, the plenitude of closed cycles." Into this natural, harmonious world of rythmic tides and ephemeral patterns, contemporary man intrudes, a violent and discordant menace. His whining dog, foul epithets, static-producing radio, gleaming knife blade and silver coins are at odds with the soothing colors and peaceful sounds of the sea and beach, where the defenseless turtle is ruthlessly disembowled, every last egg torn from her belly and offered for sale. The destruction of the natural world and its creatures is the price Mexico now pays as the human population struggles to keep bread on the table.

The crushing reality of Mexico's poverty, and the inability of the country to improve the substandard living conditions that prevail, concern the last author featured in this section: Ethel Krauze. In her novel *Donde las cosas vuelan* (Where Things Fly, 1984), two middle-aged intellectuals—a well-known male journalist and a distinguished woman sociologist/diplomat—travel to the country's northern border to conduct interviews with poor people who have migrated there in search of work. They are accompanied by the journalist's young female assistant, who is also his lover and the narrator of the story. The excerpt we have chosen culminates with the unleashing of powerful emotions triggered by the group's trip across the border, where manicured lawns and clean streets mock any hope of a better future for Mexico.

In the final section of the anthology we present eight stories whose authors explore the inner recesses of the mind and heart and the outer boundaries of our capacity to suffer and survive. Some of these writers employ fantasy, others popular culture, still others interior monologue to show the many ways in which human beings create, destroy, lie, tell the truth, transcend, succumb, live or die. Each of these texts offers a unique vision of what it means to be human in an imperfect world. Angelina Muñiz-Huberman, winner of the Villaurrutia Prize for fiction, and professor of Comparative Literature at the National Autonomous University of Mexico, opens the section. Her story "Abbreviated World" is a dark fairy tale about the horrors of the Holocaust and the cremation of Jewish children by the Nazis in which the radiant innocence and indestructible spirit of the young victims ultimately triumphs over evil and blinds the monsters who stoke the killing fires. Safe beyond an abbreviated world of torture and unspeakable horror, the children enter a new paradise in which multicolored butterflies abound and where beauty, art, and laughter may once again take root.

The inimitable Elena Poniatowska, founder and consummate practitioner of "testimonial literature," is the author of two seminal works of non-fiction: *La noche de Tlatelolco* about the 1968 massacre of student demonstrators by government troops in the Plaza of the Three Cultures, and *Nada, nadie: Las voces del temblor* about the victims of the earthquake which devastated downtown sections of Mexico City in 1987. In addition she has published several profound, best-selling novels–*Lilus Kikus; Flor de Lis; Hasta no verte Jesús mío; Querido Diego, te abraza Quiela; Tinísima*– and a critically acclaimed collection of short stories, *De noche vienes* (You Come at Night, 1979). From this last work we have chosen the final section of "Herbolario," titled "Estado de sitio" (State of Siege). In it we hear the anguished monologue of a woman who feels compelled to roam the city's streets hoping passers-by will acknowledge her existence, remember her face, as she cannot help but remember each of theirs. Is this obsessed, loving yet unrequited narrator a thinly-veiled representation of the author herself? Like the narrator, Poniatowska is known to crinkle her nose when she laughs, and she has stated unequivocally, "I write to belong." There can be no doubt that this remarkable writer belongs, not only to Mexico, but to all communities in which human dignity and compassion are upheld as treasured values.

An urgent need to receive validation and solace from a seemingly indifferent source is also the premise of Guadalupe Dueñas' "Guardian Angel" from *Antes del silencio* (1984). As if confiding in a friend, Dueñas' narrator describes her belief in the existence of an angel assigned by God to watch over her and keep her from harm. Disappointed that he has not been a more faithful companion during her unhappy life, the narrator goes on to address the angel directly, chiding him for his inconstant care, and begging him not to deny her his protection as she prepares, in the story's final sentence, to die.

An untimely and tragic death is also the focus of the story by novelist and essayist María Luisa Puga. Published in *Accidentes* (1981), and based on an item which appeared in a London newspaper—the author has lived in Europe and Africa—"Young Mother" is a wrenching interior monologue of a woman in the throes of post-partum depression. Trapped beneath an airless dome, divided against herself, unable to reconcile her desperate feelings with words spoken by friends, relatives, nurses, and the father of her newborn daughter, Puga's narrator presents a very different view of motherhood than that offered in 1937 by Nelly Campobello. In Puga's universe, madness, violence and gore are not confined to spaces outside the four walls of a lovingly-tended home, but instead poison the mind and heart of the mother herself.

When Martha Cerda wrote "Birthday," perhaps she had in mind the drawings of José Guadalupe Posada, whose charming skeletons dance, drink, laugh, and carouse long after their bodies have been laid to rest. This succinct tale of a wife who tries to seek revenge on her philandering husband from beyond the grave is from *Las mamás, los pastores y los hermeneutas* (1995), and combines the latest technology—an efficient new security system—with popular folk tradition, a powerful influence in every aspect of Mexico's cultural production. Similarly, novelist and poet Aline Petterson mines the rich vein of popular belief systems and superstition to create Águeda, the confusedly devout miracle worker of "Beyond the Gaze." From the collection of the same name *(Más allá de la mirada,* 1992), the story unfolds on two planes: scenes from Águeda's conscious, day to day life in a dusty rural village—a dizzy spell, a healing session, her cautionary tales of encounters with the devil—alternate with free-flowing interior monologues in which sexual imagery abounds. As the two planes draw closer together, and a green-eyed stranger shows up in town, the source of Águeda's misguided religious fervor is revealed, and the futility of trying to repress the past is underscored.

The impulse to escape one's past through deception also interests Angelina Muñiz-Huberman, the writer with whom we opened this section. "The Swallows of Cuernavaca" tells the story of David, an elderly Spanish-born writer who, in the pleasant garden of his small but comfortable home, regularly trades war stories and gets drunk with Alan, a veteran of the Lincoln Brigade, and Primitivo, a gardener who fought alongside Emiliano Zapata during the Mexican Revolution. Convinced that he should document for posterity his own considerable role as a combatant in several major conflicts of the twentieth century, David decides to begin writing his memoirs as soon as a pair of swallows return to nest in his garden, as they have every year since his wife left him. But when the swallows fail to return on schedule, David wonders if the birds know something that he has yet to realize: perhaps he is already dead, and no longer needs to sustain the lies he has told to himself and others for so many years.

We close our anthology with a story that in many ways echoes the collection's opening piece. Like Nelly Campobello's young alter ego, the narrator of "A Concealing Nakedness" by Nedda G. de Anhalt is threatened by a perverse monster. But while Campobello presents a villain drawn from real life (that is, the nightmare of the Revolution) de Anhalt offers an erotic fairy tale in which a woman outsmarts and kills her would-be rapist. As she realizes she has survived and prepares to face her next challenge, de Anhalt's heroine smiles enigmatically. This telling detail brings to mind Campobello's child-narrator, who upon reading of General Rueda's execution, sends "a child's smile" to the soldiers who "held in their hands my pistol withits hundred bullets disguised as the carbines resting against their shoulders." Across time and space, it seems, Campobello and de Anhalt nod to one another as they acknowledge the raw emotions and fierce spirit of women and girls who refuse to be crushed by evil.

* * *

This collection gathers varied and exquisite texts by Mexican women whose voices reach across borders. They are vulnerable and daring, introspective and surreal texts, but above all they are expressive and original, constant explorations of identity and of what it means to be Mexican, what it means to be a woman.

We hope this anthology will be another precious link in the beautiful and passionate history of Mexican culture and its people. All the writers who appear in this anthology are bold, defiant, and free despite the cultural constraints imposed on them by a patriarcal and often dogmatic society. They speak up, they invent worlds beyond the horizons of the imagination and the concrete. They recreate literary language in order to explain their own history to themselves. They return to the mythic past, undo it, retie it, but most of all they look at it with the hearts and minds of women steeped in their art. These stories do not trivialize everyday experience but rather make it part of a wider history in which the minority discourse of women now offers a singularly valuable, truly original vision. In this way, the literature of Mexican women occupies an unquestioned place of honor at the expressive and interpretive level of the other, creating common ground within the realms of history, literature, and the lives of women.

I.
RECOLLECTIONS OF THINGS TO COME

AN EXCERPT FROM
CARTUCHO

NELLY CAMPOBELLO

GENERAL RUEDA

A tall man with a blond mustache. He spoke forcefully. He had come into the house with ten men and was insulting Mama, saying, "Do you claim you're not a Villa partisan? Do you deny that? There are firearms here. If you don't give them to us, along with the money and the ammunition, I'll burn your house down!" He walked back and forth in front of her as he spoke. One of the men with him was named Lauro Ruiz (from the town of Balleza). They all shoved and bullied us. The man with the blond mustache was about to hit Mama when he said, "Tear the place apart. Look everywhere."

They poked their bayonets into everything, pushing my little brothers and sisters toward Mama, but he wouldn't allow us to get close to her. I rebelled and went over to her, but he gtave me a shove and I fell down. Mama didn't cry. She told them to do what they pleased but not to touch her children. Even with a machine gun, she couldn't have fought them all. The soldiers stepped on my brothers and sisters and broke everything. Since they didn't find firearms, they carried off what they wanted, and the blond man said, "If you complain, I'll come back and burn your house down." Mama's eyes, grown large with revolt, did not cry. They had hardened, reloading the rifle barrel of her memory.

I have never forgotten that picture of my mother, back up against the wall, eyes fixed on the black table, listening to the insults. That blond man, too, had been engraved in my memory every since.

Two years later, we went to live in Chihauhua. One day, I saw him again. He was going up the steps of the government palace. He had a smaller mustache. That day everything was ruined for me. I couldn't study. I spent the day thinking about being a man, having my own pistol, and firing a hundred bullets into him.

Another time, I saw him in the window of the palace with some people. He was laughing with his mouth open, and his mustache was shaking. I don't want to say what I saw him do, nor what he said, because you'd never believe me. Again I dreamed of having a pistol.

One day, here in Mexico City, I saw a photograph in a newspaper with this caption: "General Alfredo Rueda Quijano, before a summary court martial." It was the same blond man. His mustache was even smaller. Mama was no longer with us. She hadn't been sick, but one day, back in Chihuahua, she closed her eyes and remained asleep. I know she was tired of hearing the 30.30s. The newspaper said they were going to shoot him, here in the capital, on that very day. Some people felt sorry for him, admired him, and made a big scene over his impending death, shouting just as he had shouted at Mama the night of the attack.

The soldiers who fired at him held my pistol with its hundred bullets.

All night long, I kept saying to myself, "They killed him because he abused Mama, because he was bad to her." Mama's hardened eyes were mine now, and I repeated, "He was bad to Mama. That's why they shot him."

When I saw the picture on the front page of the Mexico City newspapers the next day, I sent a child's smile to those soldiers who held in their hands my pistol with its hundred bullets disguised as the carbines resting against their shoulders.

Translated by Doris Meyer

Recollections
of Things to Come

Elena Garro

Several days passed and the figure of Ignacio as I see it now, suspended from the uppermost branch of a tree, breaking the morning light as a ray of sunshine shatters the light in a mirror, gradually departed from us. We never spoke of him again. After all, his death only meant that there was one less Indian. We did not even remember the names of his four friends. We knew that before long other anonymous Indians would occupy their places in the trees. Only Juan Cariño persisted in not crossing any streets: locked in his room, he refused to look at me. Without his walks, the evenings were not the same, and my sidewalks were full of fruit husks, peanut shells, and ugly words.

Luchi's house was still closed when the Moncada boys

returned to town. Their arrival filled us with excitement. They walked about gaily, and as they crossed my streets they left laughter and shouting everywhere. Felipe Hurtado accompanied them.

"They seem like brothers," Matilde said as she watched them laughing and talking, all chattering at once.

"Isabel, don't interrupt!" Nicolás yelled, as he in turn interrupted his sister.

The young girl answered the rebuke with a hearty laugh which the others found contagious. It was Sunday and there was a gathering at doña Matilde's. Trays of cold drinks and sweets circulated freely, and the guests, in their best clothing, talked about the latest news and the political situation.

"Calles is going to try to get reelected," someone said almost frivolously.

"That's unconstitutional," the doctor interposed.

"Effective suffrage, no reelection!" Tomás Segovia remarked pedantically, glancing at Isabel. She paid no attention to him and went on laughing with Hurtado and her brothers. Conchita and the pharmacist tried to catch some random words from that gay conversation which seemed likely to last all night.

"Oh, I think they're talking about the lovers," Segovia said, making what he thought was a sophisticated gesture.

The young people and Hurtado looked at him uncomprehendingly.

"Who?"

"Do you know what that woman did last night?" doña Elvira asked, overjoyed that she had a chance to talk about Julia again.

"What did she do?"

"She got drunk," Conchita's mother said smugly.

"Oh, let her alone," Nicolás said impatiently.

The ladies protested. How could Nicolás dare to say such a thing when she did not let us alone? We lived in a state of perpetual unrest as a result of her whims.

"She is so pretty that any of our men would gladly change places with the General."

A storm of feminine protests greeted Nicolás' words.

"You've seen her at close range, Señor Hurtado. Is she really as pretty as they say?" doña Elvira asked, annoyed.

Hurtado thought for a minute. Then, looking into the widow's eyes and weighing his words carefully, he declared: "Señora, I have never seen a more beautiful woman than Julia Andrade."

He paused. Silence greeted his words. No one dared to ask him how and when he had learned her full name, because in Ixtepec we knew her only as Julia. The conversation became strained after the stranger's involuntary admission. His friends felt that they had inadvertently induced him to say something he should not have said.

"Why is everyone so sad?" Nicolás said, trying to enliven the group.

"Sad?" the others asked, surprised.

They could hear the military band playing marches in the plaza.

"Let's go to the serenade," Juan Moncada proposed.

"Then we can see Julia." And Nicolás rose, encouraging the others to follow.

When they reached the plaza, the serenade was well underway. Installed in the bandstand, the military band filled the air with lilting marches. The men walked to the left, the women to the right. They would circle like that for three hours, glancing at each other as they passed. Isabel and Conchita separated from the young men. The ladies, accompanied by the doctor, sat down on a bench.

The officers, each escorting his mistress, were the only ones who broke the pattern. The women were attired as usual, with their light dresses, lustrous hair, and gold jewelry. They seemed to belong to another world. Julia's presence filled the hot night air with foreboding. Her pale pink dress announced her nocturnal beauty from afar. Indifferent, with just a hint of a smile on her lips, she walked at the side of Francisco Rosas, the watchful.

"He's jealous!" we said maliciously.

The General seemed uneasy: with his yellow eyes full of dark images, he stood very erect and tried to conceal his anxiety and to find the source of the danger that threatened him. Hurtado's arrival at the plaza with the Moncada family startled him. Julia did not alter her expression. She moved among the people like a somnambulist, dazzling us with her translucent skin, her dark hair, holding her fan of finest straw in the shape of a transparent, bloodless heart. She took several turns around the plaza, and then went to sit on her accustomed bench, forming an island of light. In the center of this magic circle, surrounded by the mistresses and escorted by uniformed men, Julia seemed to be caught in a last melancholy splendor. The branches cast flickering blue shadows on her face. Someone brought drinks from Pando's cantina. The General leaned forward to serve her.

The uneasy men walking round and round the plaza hurried to come to the place where Julia was. They could not lose her: they had only to follow the aura of vanilla that clung to her.

Vainly they censured her from a distance, because once in her presence, they could not escape her mysterious attraction. When Felipe Hurtado passed he lowered his eyes as if it pained him to look at her. He scarcely replied to the words of his friends.

On nights when Julia did not leave the hotel, the plaza languished. The men waited until very late, and when they were convinced she was not going to come, they returned home feeling cheated.

That was one of the last nights we ever saw her. She was sad. She had lost weight: her nose looked sharper, paler. She gave an impression of sorrow and detachment. Submissively she let her lover take charge and arrange the straws so she could drink her beverage. Melancholically she waved her straw fan and looked at Francisco Rosas .

"I wonder why she doesn't love him" Isabel mused, watching the couple from a distance.

"Who knows!" Conchita replied, seeking out Nicolás with her eyes; he in turn was spying on Julia from a corner of the park, apparently trying to capture her transparent image for all time. Conchita blushed. Like all the young girls in Ixtepec, she secretly envied Julia. She approached her with something akin to fear, feeling herself ugly and stupid, knowing that Julia's radiance diminished her own beauty. Despite her humiliation, fascinated by love, she came close to her superstitiously, hoping that some of the beauty would rub off on her.

"I wish I were Julia!" Isabel exclaimed vehemently.

"Don't be crude!" Conchita replied, shocked by her friend's words, although she too had wished the same thing many times.

Doña Ana Moncada observed the love object with delight,

sharing her children's unreserved admiration.

"You can't deny that she has something." she said to her friend.

Señora Montúfar look at her reproachfully. "Ana, don't say such a thing! All she has is vice."

"No, no. She's not only pretty, she has something else."

Doña Elvira grew angry. Her eyes sought out her daughter and her hands signaled her to come. The young girls came to their mothers.

"Sit down and don't look at that woman any more!" Conchita's mother ordered.

"But Elvira, we all see her. She is so pretty!"

"At night, all painted up, she isn't bad, but you should see her when she wakes up with all her vices showing."

"Julia's beauty has nothing to do with the clock," Hurtado said, having joined the group. For several days he had seemed to be exasperated. He observed the love object from a distance, watching her consume her drink, outlined against a tree, under the close vigil of Francisco Rosas, and his face darkened.

"You're in love with Julia," Nicolás said in a low voice.

As if someone had suddenly said something intolerable, Felipe Hurtado left the group and strode out of the square without a word. Nicolás watched him go. He looked at doña Elvira bitterly and remembered Julia sitting on the hotel balcony with her face washed and her skin fresh as a piece of fruit. Doña Elvira's anger was natural. For him, as for Hurtado and all Ixtepec, Julia was the personification of love. Before he went to sleep, he often thought indignantly of the general who possessed that woman so unlike other women, so unreal. Hurtado's departure provoked by his words and doña Elvira's, seemed to prove he was right. He looked obliquely at his mother's friend. "She is old and ugly," Nicolás thought virulently, taking his irritation at the stranger's sudden departure out on her.

Julia's sadness seemed to infect the whole group and spread through the square. The branches cast black lace shadows that wrote maleficent signs on the officers' faces, suddenly grown sad.

Groups of men in white, leaning against the trunks of the tamarinds, uttered prolonged "ays" that lacerated the night. There is nothing easier for my people than that quick show of grief. Despite the trumpets and cymbals that made a golden explosion of sound in the bandstand, the music swirled about in pathetic spirals.

The General stood up and turned to Julia, and the two of them left the circle of friends. We saw them go away, cross the street, enter the hotel. A different light enveloped them. It was as if we could see that Julia had alienated herself from him forever.

Before the concert ended the General came out again. He was very pale and went directly to Pando's cantina without stopping at the plaza.

"He came in drunk and they were awake all night long," don Pepe whispered to the curious the next day. "The more he loves her, the more aloof she becomes. Nothing pleases her, neither the jewels nor the delicacies. She's inaccessible. I've seen the boredom in her eyes when he comes close to her. And I've also seen him sitting on the edge of the bed, watching her sleep."

"Do you love me, Julia?"

Standing by his mistress, with his coat open and his eyes downcast, the General asked the question a thousand times. She turned her melancholy eyes to him and smiled.

"Yes, I love you very much."

"But don't say it like that..."

"How do you want me to say it?" she asked with the same indifference.

"I don't know, but not like that."

A silence fell between them. Still motionless, Julia went on smiling. The General, on the other hand, trying to find something that would amuse her, paced back and forth.

"Would you like to go riding?" he asked, thinking that it had been a long time since they had taken the horses out at night, and longing for a gallop through the open country.

"If you wish."

"What do *you* want, Julia? What would please you? Ask me for something!"

"Nothing, nothing at all. I'm just fine."

And she huddled silently in a corner of the bed. He wanted to ask her to tell him what was in her memory, but he did not dare. He was afraid of what she would say.

"Do you know I live just for you?" he confessed humbly.

"I know." And Julia made a face to cheer him.

"Would you die with me, Julia?"

"Why not?"

The General left the room without saying a word. He was going to have a drink. Then he would have more courage to talk to her. As he went out he said to don Pepe, "See that the señorita does not leave her room or talk to anyone."

The instructions to don Pepe became more and more strict.

"The señorita's balcony is not to be opened!"

Julia's balcony was closed for a time, and she did not come out to the serenades on Thursdays and Sundays. We waited for her in the plaza in vain.

Translated by Ruth L. C. Simms

THE TRUE STORY
OF A PRINCESS

INÉS ARREDONDO

Seated beside her father's throne, the little princess embroidered in silence, or pretended to embroider, as she listened to matters of state presented to the king by messengers from nearby dominions.

One day, while speaking with his daughter about politics, the king was overjoyed to discover that she had become fluent in the various languages of their neighbors, friend and foe alike. So he ordered a great banquet be prepared, a feast worthy of a powerful and very beloved sovereign, at which he and his only daughter spent hours discussing matters of public policy.

But the joy of both the king and the little princess was short lived: her father died very suddenly at a young age.

Soon the widowed queen found consolation in the arms of the

prime minister, and she married him. They had a son. Deeply in love with her new husband and their baby boy, the queen forgot the princess altogether.

The queen ignored her daughter until her husband mentioned that the little princess spent hours talking with her father's old advisors, as well as merchants from far and near, and any one else who approached her. She was beloved by the people of the kingdom, who looked forward to the day she would reach the age specified by law, and assume power as her father's only heir.

The more popular the young girl became, the more her stepfather and mother hated her. The queen, blinded by passion for the prime minister, hoped that their son would become king.

Evil emotions fester like open wounds, and if left unchecked, can cause a mother to sell her child into slavery. When the daughter of one of her ladies in waiting died, the queen bribed and threatened the woman. She ordered the dead girl waked and mourned as if she were the princess, while under the cloak of dark night, she turned the real princess over to slave traders. The vile mother imposed only one condition on the dealers in human lives: that her daughter be sold in a place far, far away, where no one would recognize her.

The princess tried to look her mother in the eyes, but the queen avoided her gaze. Then the young girl lifted her head, and without looking back, joined the other slaves in the darkness.

Time passed, and the city where the princess was enslaved was defeated by foreigners in a bloody and fiery battle. The princess was among the gifts offered by the local leaders to the victors. She stood out for her bearing and beauty, and very quickly her new masters came to appreciate her talent for learning languages, their own and many others.

The captain of the foreigners soon made the princess his constant companion. As he waged a hundred battles and achieved a hundred victories, she was his translator and advisor in his dealings with those he defeated.

And in the midst of all the battles and treaties, the captain and the princess fell in love and had a son who brought them much joy during restful moments.

But the captain noticed a cloud of sadness falling like a veil over the princess' eyes whenever he held the baby in his arms He asked her many times what was wrong, until one day she told him her story.

The captain ordered his troops to head to the kingdom from which the princess had been taken. The kings, queens, and nobles of the region knew the captain's army was invincible, so they surrendered without a fight. The troops easily reached the border of the princess' kingdom, where her stepbrother and mother were summoned, as the prime minister had already died.

The next day, the captain and the princess found the queen and her son kneeling in the dust, crying and trembling with fear. The mother could not deny the princess' story, because she and her daughter looked very much alike, and perhaps her conscience had long troubled her for the terrible thing she had done. When she saw the princess standing next to the captain, she assumed they would kill her and began to cry and tremble even more, unable to lift her head.

But without hesitation, the princess descended the stairs to hug her mother and stepbrother. She raised them from the dusty ground to their feet, wiped their faces with her handkerchief, and gave them splendid gifts: food, jewels, clothing, anything at hand.

Once calm, the mother and her son admitted that the kingdom belonged to the princess, and wished with all their hearts to give it back to her. But the princess refused to take the kingdom, as she knew she had her own destiny to fulfill. She let her mother and stepbrother go in peace, forgiven and happy. But she was the happiest of all.

Many thousands of years ago the same thing happened in Egypt to Joseph and his brothers, as the Bible tells us. This almost identical story took place in Mexico less than five hundred years ago.

Yes, the princess was called La Malinche and the Captain was Hernán Cortés.

Translated by Nancy Abraham Hall

II.
COATLICUE SWEPT

Regarding My Mestiza Self

Marcela Guijosa

How easy it could have been. A pretty and complete blend. Like the story about the races: God puts little human figures in the oven, and some come out undercooked, and they're the white race. The better ones are dark, nice and golden, well done. Us.

As if God had kneaded Indian dough with Spanish dough, mixed them together into a single mass, then popped it in the oven. And the Mexican batch came out just right. All one shade, the color of coffee with cream.

If only the Spaniards had arrived, not killed anyone, and conversed with the Indians. If only they had agreed, and each Spanish man had paired up with an Indian woman, and vice-versa. Choose a girlfriend or boyfriend. Have children. Let's create a new race.

And if all of us had Spanish great-grandfathers and Indian

great-grandmothers, and we remembered them fondly, and venerated them equally, the two original, mythical races that gave us life, father of our flesh, mother of our flesh. If the two separate cultures lived on only in our memory, and our Mexican culture had preserved, and practiced daily the best of both worlds, now fused and kneaded, and inseparable.

If only I weren't this poorly- made hodgepodge, with lumps of white flour and clumps of brown sugar that hurt me. If only I were all one color. If my dreams and my gods didn't tear me apart, tugging at me from shores separated by a vast sea of solitude.

If my pyramids were completely mine, and if I understood the old language and the old rituals and the terrible plumed serpents and the skulls that watch me in a language I don't know.

If the cathedrals didn't weigh so heavily on me, stones shamelessly stolen from another religion. If I didn't carry such a heavy cross along ground strewn with cacti and entrails, my knees torn to shreds, my hands pierced by thorns, so as to see my Virgin of Guadalupe.

If I didn't have separate roots that threaten to split my trunk in two. If my feet weren't standing on such distant parcels of earth, my genitals sore and split, half over there, half over here, my womb open, my legs stretched at strange angles, always off balance.

Or my body and soul so far apart, so different, my flesh of this land, this water, and these volcanoes, yet my spirit so invaded by Latin words, and ballads, and Punic Wars and theological tomes.

If I only knew who I was without wearing a *huipil* and a *quesquémetl* one day, and a lovely silk or laced-edged piqué blouse the next, because after all, colorful embroidery and hand-loomed cotton belts are fine, but only if you're headed to Cuernavaca on a Saturday, or you work at the Colegio de México or the Museum of Anthropology, and they're having an *amusgo* or Guatemalan *huipil* contest. But underneath it all, you're a middle class woman who can't afford the outfits you really like, certainly not clothes designed for wealthy, respectable people, or at least those considered respectable, linen suits and pure silk blouses, or blouses edged in lace like your grandmother used to make. And you're not a *tehuana* walking around in an embroidered top, long flowered skirt, and antique necklace because you live in Mexico City today, in the postmodern age, and when you show up in villages in native dress, the Indian women look down on you and even insult you for wearing clothes that aren't really your own. With your hair cut short, almost shaven, and your denim jeans, no matter how many San Pablito blouses and silver earrings you wear, you're half and half, a hybrid, split in two, a mermaid with the face of a woman, breasts, feminine arms and polished nails, and at the same time a blind, irrational, underwater animal, with cold and ancient blue-scaled flesh that smells of fish, unable to walk on land where you must live in order to survive, half air and half water, half sun and half shade, half cold and half warmth.

And so you are totally half and half, half Christian and half pagan and magical and idolatrous. Half masculine and half feminine, half free, active and brave, a conqueror, an adventurer, an evangelist, a teacher. Half night, moon, water and submission, dark and receptive, fecund, sleeping, cyclical. And crazy, and humid, and passive. Passive root, passive milk, passive tomb.

Translated by Nancy Abraham Hall

An Excerpt From Isomorfismos

Esther Seligson

"Nous vivons dans le torrent de la reciprocité universelle, unis a lui par un lien inefable."
—Martin Buber

Annunciation

His foot wounded, once again, on the sole, right where he was beginning to step with joy, annunciation of alchemies in perspective, ravines and deserts, with nothing to eat but some roots and tasteless *totopos* and some *teocomite* thorns that he carries in his sack as small offerings and sacrifices en route to the sanctuary. The *oactli* has already sung its song of future good omens, and there is nothing to fear. "The weak traveler who doubts merely kicks up dust along the road," his grandfather would say. There's no need to hurry. Now time is no longer an obstacle. Along another path she, too, walks, and they are bound to find each other at the moment in which they were separated, neither before nor after. To follow one's own path means the rejection of those chosen by others, he knows it, and will remain alone, against wind and tide, tremulous warrior who brandishes his sword in the air to test its weight and mettle. He will be spared not a single abyss, solitary hunter who lays a track knowing that doves will come to collect it. Similarly, she formed a circle with heaps of loose grain, and in hopes of following her own course, placed herself in the center, and set the piles on fire. She gathered a bit of the ashes in a handkerchief, a matter of ritual, who knows—it is said that the souls of the dead roll around in them so as to rid themselves of sins—, and without turning her head nor consulting omens, she headed out.

The afternoon bubbles, and flows stealthily towards the lap of night. A lukewarm sky envelops the city, like a caress on a cheek, a pleasure of solitude that relieves eyes and ears. They walk hand in hand, barely brushing one another with fingertips and palms, in a dialogue of unarticulated purity (the same purity that makes them search for each other's bare feet under the sheets, winding them together before falling asleep), similar to the silent sunset. By contrast, in photographs they hug one another, attached to an unknown yearning of unmoved perpetuity.

I heard him arrive from a place beyond Time, I saw him come without mist, his knapsack flung over his shoulder, one after-noon before nightfall, black hair, and as the poet would say, a spring-like sparkle in his dark pupils, flashes of sea in his smile. Hurriedly he kissed me on the corner of my mouth: slow-ly the fire spread through my body, so slowly that it still burns my bones, and I wander on the edges of his lips of foam like a radiant corpuscle.

I approached her from a place beyond Time, little by little. I knew that the Earth is neither enormous nor round—that's sheer imagination—and that it moves only because we never stop walking. That's how I found her, bird of a non-existent Paradise, one afternoon enraptured by the brief brush of my mouth against her cheek. I cherish the depths of desire, a sun that made me drunk and still hurts. I took her hand and offered her a bed in the pupils of my eyes...

No one would say it was a dream, even though both of them were unified from that point on, a presence of liquid light, a name that inhabits their entire skin, a name they recognize even before they voice it. Somewhere, at some point in time, there was a flower, a stone, a piece of glass, don Jesús continues, a woman swollen with waves who lives in the elbow of the stream, Lady-of-the-Star-Spangled *Huipil*, Lady-of-Our-Flesh, she who holds up the Earth and covers it with cotton. But might we not carry our own executioners within? Perhaps we enjoy seeing ourselves in the hangman and in he who betrays? Only those aware of the True Name will be sure to receive his help. The first death was a divine movement, self-immolation; the second, a murder.

The train wraps him in its scarlet and purple journey. He knows it is necessary to shun mirrors, even though they pierce his hands and eyelids—"Better to have scars than incurable wounds," Grandfather would say—so that the brilliance of the moon does not bewitch him and steal his soul, *itzpapalotl.* He knows he shouldn't force his words, making idols of them, ambulant chimeras seduced by an esthetic image of themselves. She knows that every serpent must be fought with another serpent, that every dragon hides among its scales sparkles of something inexhaustible, and, in any case, superior to fate (even though he will one day declare, three times, "I do not know her.") And the ocean gale, not the wind, will arrive to slap their faces, and mute, they will descend towards a mute hell devoid of tortures in order to deposit their offering of quail (Philortix tasciatus: *males and females of identical appearance and size, their flanks beribboned in white and black. Also known as "chorrunda"),* drops of amber and buds of jasmine. A need to incinerate oneself, with words and without them, unpostponable metamorphosis shared in the mysteries of incense and rose. They walk. Yet they still do not realize that they are distancing themselves from that which they love and loves them, but like children who, with their index fingers, follow the paths of raindrops on the windowpane, they already sense that what is real is unattainable, and what is visible grows beyond itself and stretches toward the kingdom of the invisible. He was an entranced child—that stubborn gesture as he tied his shoelaces together—eyes of a wounded deer, early awareness of his separateness from the world, not wanting it as a home so that he would not expect shelter from it. His greedy bare fingers resting on the skin of things. What abandonment, what loss drained his joy of living and left cemetery ghosts in his arms? Aunt Concepción gives immaculate roses to the Virgin, after having removed, one by one, the thorns that end up, pain and pleasure of offering, pressed into her fingertips. To bury his face in her wet hair, and fall asleep amid her prayers. To dream, perhaps, of taking apart each bead of the rosary on her nipples, and to place a constellation of saliva drops around each of her dark aureoles. She was always a child who anticipated things, believed in words yet to be spoken, in days that open to a recent now, in fairy tales. Sometimes she awoke with woodsy breezes in her hair and the amazement of finding herself a stranger to this time and world. What early banishment snatched the taste of immensity from her mouth? In her he recognized a perfume, a tenacious expectancy, perhaps the name of an unexpressed desire. In him she recognized a dream, a search, a brightness that awaits a powerful and inextinguishable irradiation.

I call you with the voice of my reunified being, and I know that you are there, an intimate night time patience that opens and makes way for light, the new light of a new dawn. I know that we weave the profile of a face that does not hide behind a veil of nostalgia. Your being is given up to my being, unique tree where the soul took root, and yet birds, fowl of time, errant and nearby, did we not find ourselves as walkers...?

Angel of the Annunciation, take my hand without reading a destiny upon it—do not yearn for what is already yours, Grandfather would say—and entwine your lines with mine, slowly, without borders, present eternity. The embrace will suffice to populate the universe. What flower that has not imbibed its share of mud shows its colors to the light?

An image is like fire. It calls from the earth and adheres to the object that is burning. Clouds pass, thin indigo lizards and reddish bugs, and the rain does its work upon the fertility of the fields. Things that are in agreement vibrate in unison and all beings flow toward their individual forms. "We live in the torrent of universal reciprocity, joined to it by an ineffable link," remarked Grandfather. The expanding crescent emerges bathed by a fearful clamor. The man who brings rain, at the top of the mountain, crag of grave mounds and oblations, looks toward the ocean where the sun is hiding. It holds in its right hand an enormous frog, and a crown of mint and parsley in its left. Messenger of the Lord-from-the-Place-Raindrops-Spring, don Jesús gives movement to the collection of tenuous and viscous threads that constitute the matter of life. "Each one receives that which is in accord with his being, what is appropriate and makes him happy. Lift up your brilliant and precious heart, turn your eyes toward Heaven. No one is tested with trials which he is incapable of surmounting, but everything arrives of its own accord at the appropriate time." To the brink of what edges does a kiss lead? Point of arrival, its touch took them by surprise. He dreams about a city of air and lets time pass while he puts his arm around the waist he has not yet touched, her sweaty waist, clasped by the imagination of his hands. She constantly pushes aside a perpetual yearning for closeness which the dream of him will carry off, along with his wanderings and forbidden orchards, in a bundle full of stars. She opens herself, stream-bed and furrow. He penetrates waves and wind, wanderer of verses. He carries islands of peace in his hands; she, a burning river-bed of windmills and storms. Snails of white sand their bodies slide until they fall, inlets on the high tide, alchemies where reality and delirium flow together, always alchemies, reservoir where they drink and bathe under the open sky, winged nuptials, until they reach themselves in the absent time that they owe as a debt to one another. "The kiss places order upon the world," concludes don Jesús.

They both retrace their steps: East, South, West, North, East. A light, persistent drizzle moistens the afternoon. Broad stoles of bruised clouds suck up the light, shiny despite the grayness. The pestilence of the lagoon rumbles in their noses, although, as consolation, at least, the swarms of mosquitoes will not bite a soul. The bell of the cathedral calls out monotonously, divining the laziness of the faithful sons of San Cuilmas Petatero, who nothing will move on this late afternoon of humid drowsiness. The smell of newly roasted coffee and warm bread is in the air. Several children kick an empty can as if it were a ball. A few umbrellas busy themselves in front of the bakery and the pulque shop. The park benches wait in vain for their lovers. "I will always love you," whisper the leaves of the trees as they continuously die. Only the condemned men remain standing in the little plaza outside the prison. "They are agitators," it is said, across their chests hang signs that describe their so-called crimes: strike, hunger strike, strike for justice, they ask for justice from the foremen with whips for whom building the Wall is in itself already a sufficient honor, why invoke other reasons which may not be those of the current strong man? Do the gods laugh? "They are the *nenonquich,* the useless men born on the good-for-nothing days, when everything is gaunt, unserviceable, ominous. Oh! We don't really live, we don't really come to last on earth," murmur the people. The *copal* burns generously on the braziers. Decapitation, flaying, dismemberment: the method doesn't really matter. What counts is the spectacle, the ceremony, the sacrament, to participate and become One with the divinity, any divinity, whichever integrates contrary powers and opposing passions, calms fears, exonerates cowardice and procrastination, and reconciles sins and mistakes. The bonfires are lit with aromatic reeds and green wood. Bones and skulls are gathered: those to be singed are placed in stacks; those that must first by ground up are tossed into a pile alongside the stone bowls. Femurs and skulls represent complete surrender, the complete turning over of the person to the god. "The body that comes back to life will be the one whose soul has put down roots, but if you rush the hour, it will make you turn back," says Grandfather. Like being born inside a seed, a seed in love. At some point in time they shared the same garden and an identical tree, they deciphered the language of the spirals of incense, they wove blue lizards, and played on the dusty trail of a comet with brightly colored almonds.

Your presence filled my room with indigo plants and goldfinches. A fecundity of a silent grotto bound my errant feet with the deeprootedness of home to your hands. I did not drink your breath, nor did I sink into your embrace: I collected my being within you. A sparkle of purity on my skin tells me that you sow my name in a verse...

And for this dawn, which is a light-filled circle of your presence, I have neither words nor garments: I surrender naked and silent to it. There are no questions. Only the slight brush of my fingers on your face.

It is love that elects us to serve in its temples, chief priests

and priestesses. We are our bodies and the reality that surrounds them: that is our divine likeness," he insists.
Come, draw near, to the full...
Come, receive me openly...

A while ago the *acachichictle* announced the impending dawn to the fishermen. Among the cattails and sedge, the messenger of the Lord of the Dawn alerted the last dreamers of the night with his caw. The dawn of gold and silver and fire reaches their two silhouettes walking along the beach still covered with night dew. Is there any pause in the movement? They are holding hands. Today the dog follows them meekly, and does not get under foot. In the estuary, the boat that they both carved is tied to the ramshackle wooden dock. She climbs aboard and places the oars, hanging to one side, in the water. At the stern he pushes off, to beyond the crest of the waves. A soft current carries them out to sea...

Translated by Nancy Abraham Hall

Glossary of Náhuatl Words
totopos: pieces of fried tortilla
teocomite: oval-shaped cactus whose thorns were used in sacrificial
rituals
oactli: bird whose song predicts happy outcomes
huipil: traditional cotton blouse worn by Indian women
itzpapalotl: nocturnal butterfly
nenonquich: men born on days considered unlucky
copal: resin used in ritual burnings
acachichictle: early-rising bird

AN EXCERPT FROM
TOO MUCH LOVE

SARA SEFCHOVICH

After that nothing more was possible. But you found more. You found the gray, strong, powerful rivers. You took me to the Usumacinta in Tenosique, to the Grijalva in Villahermosa, to the Papaloapan in Tlacotalpan, to the Coatzacoalcos in Minatitlán, to the Tonalá in La Venta, to the Pánuco, to the Bravo, and even to one made of pumice in Amatitán. We took the ferry from Mazatlán to La Paz and from Playa del Carmen to Cozumel and you took me down the rapids of the Balsas, where I saw a dog dragged by the current and a hat caught on a rock.

You took me to the open sea of Tepic and the still bay of Caleta. You showed me the tranquil waters and the blues and greens of the Caribbean and we swam in the warm sea at Zihuatanejo, gazing at the endless horizon illuminated by the afternoon sun. In Vallarta and in Campeche we walked along the sea wall, in Cancún and Caleta de Campos, in Barra de Navidad, Careyes, Mismaloya, Huatulco and Akumal we walked on beaches of powdered sand. I got to know the Nautla sand bar, the Sabancuy inlet, the San Blas canal, so thick with vegetation that barely any light could get through. We saw boiling mud at Los Azufres, natural irrigation ditches at Molcajac, waterfalls in Huautla, Sontigomostoc, Baseachic, Jumatán, Eyipantla, Juanacatlán and La Mesilla, waterfalls in Monterrey, in Avándaro and in Cuernavaca. We saw the Uruapan falls, the one in Atoyac, the ones in Cuetzalan and Misol-Ha, and swam in the freezing and transparent waters of their pools. We saw lakes in Pátzcuaro, Chapala, Zirahuén and Cuitzeo, lagoons in Jalapa and Villahermosa. We stood on the banks of Lakes Tamiahua, Necaxa and Tequesquitengo, and in San Miguel Regla and Guelatao, where they seemed like ponds. And everywhere the lagoons had names like Illusion, Dream and Enchanted.

We took a boat through Chacahua and through Coyuca while birds cried in the trees and through Celestum as flamingos flew overhead. We went through Mandinga, where there were thickets of mangrove, through Catemaco, where there were monkeys, down the River Lagartos, where there were cranes. We sailed Nichupté, Xel-Ha and Bacalar, full of fish, and the seven lagoons of Zempoala full of beer cans. I was surprised by Catazajá where the population doubles, then receeds on a seasonal basis, and by a lagoon in Puebla where hot and cold, sweet and salt water mix.

Yes, you impressed me with nature. With oceans and rivers, with waterfalls, lakes and lagoons, with natural underground reservoirs and beaches. We saw the sacred underground reservoir at Chichen-Itzá, where the water smells like blood, the one at Valladolid, inside a cave, the one at Dzinup that reaches the ocean, the one at Dzibichaltún full of children. We swam in the enormous pools at Nu-tun-tun and Ajacuba, Las Estacas, Tolantongo, Tequisquiapan, Ixtlán de los Hervores, Tzindejé, Taninul, Atzimba, Taboada, Amahac and La Caldera. We swam at Agua Blanca surrounded by the tropics and at Agua Azul in the middle of the jungle. We swam in sulphurous, hot, limpid, rough, sweet and salty springs, in water meant for drinking and waters meant for healing, in Tehacán, in Ixtapan de la Sal, in San José Purúa, in Cuautla. We swam in pools in Oaxtepec, in Cocoyoc, in Puente de Ixtla, in Amatlán and Temixco. We waded in rivulets without names all over Morelos, in free-running streams, in ponds formed by rainwater and in a small puddle full of frogs in Jiutepec.

We saw many beaches, on the open sea and in bays, some yellow, others white or gray. We saw ports full of boats loaded with sailors, fishing ports, seas puffed with anger, and sunsets that filled me with indescribable passion. We saw reefs, thickets of mangrove and shells, rocks, hot sand and blue air.

You took me to the grottos of Cacahuamilpa, and the ones in La Estrella, Loltún and Ixtepec, the ones in Monterrey which we reached by cable car, those of Juxtlahuaca with their paintings and bats, the ones at Balancanchén where we saw the water mirror, and the ones at Zapotitlán with their offerings to witches and healers. And everywhere there was darkness, moisture, strange shapes.

You took me to see canyons where the heat was heavy and the silence very thick. The one in Sumidero with trees clinging to the sides, the one in San Pedro Mártir, the Zopilote Canyon, the one in Chicoasén, those called Diablo, Lobo, Peña del Aire, Espinazo del Diablo, and the terrible ones in Baja California, deaf from the heat, full of nothing but silence. And everywhere I felt strange, deeply afraid.

I saw the desert with its sand dunes for the first time in Samalayuca, then in Torreón and Durango. You refused to cross the Altar Desert by day because you said it was haunted, and you refused to cross the Bolsón de Mapimí at night because you said there were ghosts. You spoke of arid and bare places where lost travelers went mad and died of thirst. But none of these places was like the Desert of Silencio, full of enormous turtles and hares, fossils and aerolites, stars in the sky and cacti in the sand, a place where all sound is cut off and disappears.

Yes, you wanted to impress me with nature, and you did.

I remember the volcanos, Ixtacíhatl with her lofty rocks and her falls, her views. I remember La Malinche, Pico de Orizaba, Volcán del Fuego with its fumaroles and lava, Nevado de Toluca, Paricutín, Ixtle, now dead, and Chichonal, active once again. We gazed at Paricutín from Charapan, Popcatépetl from Amecameca, and Nevado from the Valle de Bravo highway. In order to fully take in the Colima, we spent three nights out at the Hacienda San Antonio in cabins full of wandering souls and silence.

I remember the vistas you showed me. Those from the highway between Durango and Mazatlán full of waterfalls, stones and vegetation, and those from the road to La Rumorosa, full of rocks, mountains, desert and sea. I remember an oasis near Loreto, the Sierra Madre behind Nuevo León, the cliffs at the tip of Baja California, the reefs pounded by the sea on Isla Mujeres and in Palancar, the coral near Chetumal.

I remember the rocks in the Majalcá Park, with their capricious shapes, hard and rough, the enormous rocks of El Chico, the piled-up rocks in a Puebla valley, the waterless, rocky, level ground in Coahuila, the shining rocks full of minerals in Pachuca, the perfectly round rocks somewhere in Jalisco, the basaltic prisms in San Miguel Regla, the basaltic stones of Zacatecas' Sierra de los Organos, and the stoney hills surrounding Tepotzlán.

I remember the views looking up from Cuetzalan and down from San José Purúa. I remember the Valle de Apan full of maguey plants as far as the eye could see, the valley we viewed from Calpulalpan, blinded by the light, the deep green valley we saw from Xochicalco, and the one we viewed from Monte Albán.

I remember the roads around Campeche, Guanajuato and Zacatecas. I remember the hill at La Silla from which we saw Monterrey, the hill at Bufa overlooking Zacatecas, the hill at Perdices in Tabasco, the watchtower on El Espinazo in Mazatlán, and a very small spot from where one can see all of Pátzcuaro, with its steep streets and red roofs.

I remember nature with its changing moods: how it rains in the Sierra de Mixistlán, such a rugged place, and in Oaxaca's high sierra and in the thick and low-lying mountains of Huejutla, and how, by contrast, it never rains in Hidalgo's Mezquital, nor in the San Luis Desert. Because you wanted to impress me with the natural wonders of this land. That's why you took me the Barranca de Cobre, the tip of Baja California, the Caribbean Sea, and Popocatéptl. And I fell madly in love with you and with this country.

* * *

Thanks to you my eyes have been filled forever with light, water, stones, sun, earth, sky, and greeness. I will always carry within me cacti and maguey plants, laurels and palm treees, cypresses, oaks and pines. I'll always have within me flowers of a thousand colors, fruits of a thousand flavors, objects of a thousand uses, dark, sad and thin people, people of faith standing in front of their adobe shacks with roofs of palm.

Enormous valleys and sinuous mountains live within me now. I remember Sierra Tarahumara with its extremely tall trees, its deep ravines and its tumultuous waterfalls. I remember desolate spots, fog-covered woods, the desert and the hills rising everywhere, the cultivated, green fields, hours and hours on the empty roads, time standing still and our silence, the sound of the wind, the clouds, the rain, the transparent light. You and I, the quiet ones, moved, impressed, reverent.

I remember the road that runs through Baja California, watching the infinite blue ocean. At times it would leave us, and at others it was but an arm's length away. Sometimes the roads were steep mountains, and then level. There was always open, suprising beauty. The most primordial of all places, the cliffs and the rocks, both on land and in the sea. Seals, whales, gulls, the freest of animals. And at the end of the road, the turbulent, impetuous waters of San Lucas.

I remember the majestic, snow-covered volcanoes. We could see them the whole length of the wooded highway from Chalco to Tlamacas and at last, in Amecameca we had them here, in front of our eyes, with that light that exists nowhere else in the world, that light and that air, illuminated, transluscent, luminous, clear, very thin, cold and transparent. I remember the rocky walls of Ixtacíhuatl, covered with ice or bathed in falls, the views from Popocatéptl, the snow at the top of Nevado de Toluca, a crater with two lagoons and another very cold crater.

But what I most remember is the day you told me you wanted to see where the sun rose and where it set, and you took me very early to a spot between Orizaba and Toluca, and later that afternoon to a place between Citlaltépetl and Xinantécatl, your own names for the volcanoes, and we spent the rest of the day in Ozumba because you said it was there that the North Star reached its highest point.

My eyes have been filled by lagoons of crystalline water, enormous and rough rocks, turbulent seas. My eyes have been filled by mountain ranges and tropical jungles, markets, churches, corrals, mangrove swamps and shells, earthen pots, embroidered dresses. And people: so many men and women, so many old people, so many: dark, skinny and quiet children. They are, and always will be, visible to me, under my skin, thanks to you.

Our pilgramages to the holiest and most fervent places have been permanently etched within me. The sanctuary of Zapopan with its singing women, the church at Chamula with such very sad Indians, the San Luis desert and the Quemado hill with such very magical peyote. And our pilgrimages to places alive with history have been etched: where Hidalgo gave the Cry for Independence in Dolores and where they killed him in Chihuahua, where Maximilian disembarked in Veracruz and where they killed him in Querétaro, the spot to where Juárez dragged his archives and his government, where Porfirio Díaz triumphed in Puebla and the port through which he went into exile, where Zapata was born in Anenecuilco and where they killed him in Chinameca.

Of all our journeys, of all our pilgramages, I was most deeply moved when we went to Comala to look for ghosts and echoes, and when we went to Huasteca in search of Tamoanchán, where corn first grew in Paradise, and when we went across the plains of Apan, the extremely dry home of the maguey plant. But the greatest trip we took, the most important road we traveled was the one that traced the steps of the Aztecs, who left Mexcaltitlán one day, traversed every desert in their path, remained for three years in Pipiolcomic and then in Chicomostoc for who knows how long, until finally reaching Tenochtitlan. Unlike them, we did not enter the city...

* * *

At your side I came to know the thirteen skies and five suns, the five seas, the five colors and the forty-two types of corn plants. At your side I came to know the four spaces and the four times, the four elements and the four points of the compass which are earth's directions. I came to know the three mother sierras and the volcanic axis, the theological virtues of faith, hope and charity and the three cardinal virtues of intelligence, memory and will. At your side I came to know all the fruits, all the flowers and all the trees. I came to know the sound of wind and the color of light, the density of water and the lightness of earth, the thousand species of cacti that are born in this country and the thousand forms of crafts the native peoples make by hand; the three-hundred names for corn and the three-hundred twenty-five uses of the peanut. I came to know the four colors of mole, the four of sapodilla, and tasted the four types of fresh water, the three colors of young corn, the three types of bananas and the three types of prickly pear. I also came to know the many varieties of beans, the many types of chilis and herbs, the many skillful moves one can make on horseback, the many ways to cook pork, and the many, very many ways to make love.

You showed me the day-before-yesterday places where God was everywhere, and yesterday's places where God was in Heaven, and today's godless places.

At your side I learned that the maguey is sacred, that beans are sacred, and that pulque and peyote are as well. But I learned that the most sacred plant of all is corn. That's why images of Christ are made from stalks and the first human beings were made of corn. Corn, source of life and its grace, food of the gods and of men, sacred grain, divine plant, our flesh, you were born in Tamoanchán.

Along every road and in every place we saw corn, we saw maguey plants and beans, we saw sugar cane, we saw fruit. From high atop the volcanic cone of Xihuingo we saw the maguey-filled plains of Apan and I felt an enormous love for this country   From the hights of Telapon and El Tláloc, I saw everything a human being is able to see and I felt an enormous love for you and for this my country, country of hills and volcanoes, of corn fields and maguey plants, of colors and sounds, of native peoples and gods.

Translated by Nancy Abraham Hall

An Excerpt from
Shipwreck Syndrome

Margo Glantz

Coatlicue swept as the serpents on her skirt rested. One day she found a large feather, looked at it with curiosity and tucked it in her bosom. After a mythical amount of time the feather became a robust baby boy who threatened to come forth from her womb fully clothed, headdress and all, like Cupid, the god of love and childhood. But Coyolxauhqui, the moon goddess, daughter of the earth and sister of the sun, the moon and the stars, the one with small bells on her face, developed her own incestuous and profound hatred of her mother and brother, and denounced them to her four hundred southern siblings, the Centzon-Huitznaua.

This denunciation results in the guillotine. The god of war decapitates his sister and throws her off a cliff while her four hundred siblings become stars. Coyolxauhqui turns up artfully torn to pieces, vestiges dulled by a beautiful shade of red. Her legs are tucked up coquettishly, and on her Aztec feet she displays a pair of divinely elegant huaraches. Her breasts hang easily and her writhing recalls the sound of the small bells that she loved so much. Her deadly brother, the left-handed hummingbird, leads his armies into war: it is the sun that cuts off the head of the moon and causes the stars to flee. A traffic light is lit in the main temple indicating required stops for the dwarfish cars leaving the area. Some idols still hold the blue remnants of precolombian water, and from sockets of conch, they gaze with obsidian eyes at the cradles that stunt the growth of aristocratic children. Next to them stands the goddess Tiamat, destroyed from the inside by her children, and from her torn body emerge the Assyrian myths of heaven and earth.

Translated by Nancy Abraham Hall

An Excerpt From
Balún Canán

Rosario Castellanos

Whenever the Indians of Chactajal come to the house, it's a sign there's a fiesta on the way. They bring sacks of maize and beans, bundles of salt beef and cones of brown sugar. Then the granaries are opened and the rats run about again, fat and sleek

Lounging in the hammock on the veranda, my father receives the Indians. They aproach, one by one, and offer their foreheads for him to touch with the three middle fingers of his right hand. Then they return to the respectful distance where they belong. My father talks to them about the business of the farm. He knows their language and their customs. They answer respectfully in words of one syllable, laughing briefly when they're supposed to.

I go to the kitchen, where Nana is heating coffee.

"They've brought bad news, like the black moths."

I sniff in the larder. I like to see the color of the butter and to touch the bloom of the fruit, and peel the onion-skins.

"It's witches' doings that's afoot, child. They gobble everything up—the crops, peace in the family, people's health."

I've discovered a basket of eggs. The freckled ones are turkeys'.

"Just look what they've done to me."

Pulling up her *tzec,* Nana shows me a soft reddish wound disfiguring her knee.

I stare at it, eyes wide with surprise.

"Don't say anything about it, child. I came away from Chactajal hoping they wouldn't follow, but their curse reaches a long way."

"Why do they hurt you?"

"Because I was brought up in your house. Because I love your parents and Mario and you."

"It's wicked to love us?"

"It's wicked to love those that give orders and have possessions. That's what the law says."

The cauldron rests quietly on the coals. Inside it the coffee has begun to boil.

"Tell them to come. Their drink's ready."

I go away, sad because of what I've just heard. My father dismisses the Indians with a gesture and lies on in the hammock, reading. I see him now for the first time. He's the one who gives the orders and owns things. I can't bear the look of him and run to take shelter in the kitchen. The Indians sitting by the hearth are holding their steaming mugs very gingerly. Nana serves them with such measured courtesy one would think they were kings. On their feet they wear sandals—and thick cakes of mud; and their breeches of unbleached cotton are patched and dirty, and their food-bags are empty.

When she's finished serving them, Nana sits down too. Solemnly she stretches both hands to the fire and holds them there a while. They talk, and it's as if a circle had closed around them. I break it in my suffering.

"Nana, I'm cold."

She draws me to her lap, as she always has done ever since I was born. It is warm and tender, but it has a wound. A wound, and it's we who've opened it.

Translated by Irene Nicholson

III.
WHERE THINGS FLY

Sunday

Silvia Molina

For Hernán Lara Zavala

A fresh morning breeze moves the curtains, and blows through the crack of the window to the bed. It's still dark, but the sun is starting to come up because I can hear the birds warbling from the laurel bushes in the plaza across from the hotel; I don't know what kind of birds they are: some people call them thrushes; others say crows or starlings, even magpies. I call them birds. The blue-black birds in the laurel bushes wake up automatically. They can't be cold, they must be hungry.

I slept all night, yet I'm tired. Instead of dragging myself over to shut the window, I pull the covers to my chin. I reach toward Alfonso, but the sheets are icy cold. He must have gone out for a walk along the sea wall because I don't hear any noise in the bathroom. I've been watching him, and he gets by with less and less sleep.

I'm cold and I wish I could go back to sleep. I pull Alfonso's pillow toward me. It still holds the unmistakable scent of his hair, of his large, trim body. I think about him. I've memorized everything about him, especially his hands and the wrinkles on his face that tell me all about his character, his personality, the experience he has drawn from life. I imagine him still turning me on , wrapping me in his arms and legs to warm me up, heating my body.

Again I tell myself that Alfonso has gone out for a walk along the sea wall, and I'm afraid. I don't like to be alone in an unfamiliar room, in a city that isn't my own. I don't like to be alone when I'm with him, although I'm not exactly with him: knowing he's nearby is reassuring.

The warbling of the birds flutters around the plaza. Maybe Alfonso sat down on a sea wall bench to watch the ocean at dawn. Maybe he went downstairs, discreetly, to use the phone.

I never used to be afraid of being alone. I never believed in ghosts and I was at ease with the usual nighttime noises: creaking doors, barking strays, air bubbles in the pipes, the factory whistle; but after Ruben and I separated, something changed. I felt insecure in the apartment, and anxious when I'd get home from work at night, to the point where I would leave a light on all day so I wouldn't have to face the dark with its worrisome shadows and silences. That's why as soon as I'd get in I would turn on the radio or the record player or the television, and for added security I put an extra lock on the front door and a small peephole through which I could check out anyone who rang the doorbell. But you get used to anything. I eventually got over my fear. I don't know why I allow it now. Maybe I'm afraid that this Sunday will end or go by too quickly. I don't understand it. I don't dare say that I'm afraid Alfonso won't come back. I know he loves me; I'm sure, even though it took me a while.

On Sundays I used to wake up next to Ruben as if I had slept peacefully alongside my brother. He'd go buy the newspaper at the corner stand while I made breakfast, and then we'd both eat in silence.

I'd like to go for a walk, I would say as I sipped my orange juice and he drank in the Ovations and Esto sports pages. Soccer was his passion. I'd like to go for a walk, I'd insist, while he watched the game on television. I'd like to go for a walk, and frustrated, I'd give up while he stayed in the apartment watching a movie on the VCR.

Sundays with Ruben I felt trapped in a tedious world. Relaxed Sundays, Ruben used to call them.

The breeze reaches me again. Maybe there's a storm in the port. I get up to close the window and I look out to see if Alfonso is in the plaza or out on what I can glimpse of the sea wall. I don't find him.

The sun is up; he'll be back soon. I look at myself in the mirror and brush my hair: I find a gray one, and feel proud of the small white tuft that's beginning to show above my forehead: now I won't look a lot younger than Alfonso when we're together.

I'm glad he didn't see me wake up. My reflection in the mirror shows traces of sleep. I go wash my face with cold water, get rid of the pastiness, and return to the bed; it's too early to get up.

I remember when my mother used to wake me up on Sundays

so I could take a bath, get dressed and put my hair in a pony tail. Then she and my father would take me to Mass at San Francisco's. Afterward we'd have breakfast at the Paris Cafe or the Tacuba Cafe, which my father always chose because that's what his father did. Those were coffee-with-milk Sundays; the only occasions when I was allowed to order coffee with milk, and dunk a sweet bread in it. We used to walk through Alameda Park as if it were the one in San Diego where my mother grew up. They always bought me a balloon or cotton candy that melted in my mouth while they strolled hand in hand. I think we were happy then. Things weren't rushed: it would get late, and then we'd have to take a taxi to my grandparents' house in Tlalpan. I'd climb trees to pick green olives that my mother boiled in sugar water. Grandfather used to teach me the colors and names of the plants he grew in the orchard behind the house:

"Carnation, red; agapanthus, blue; daisy, yellow," he said, naming each flower in turn.

And later, while Grandfather and Dad talked, and Mom and Grandmother knit, I played with the children in the neighborhood. Sometimes we'd spend the day at Xochimilco with relatives visiting from out of town. We'd eat on one of the boats, then wander through the marketplace. Some mornings we'd end up at the Shrine to the Virgin of Guadalupe because my mother had insisted.

Other Sundays, I used to wake up early, get picked up by a group of friends from the university, and spend the day out in the country exploring towns in Morelos or Mexico State, where we'd visit colonial churches and landmarks, and stroll through parks. We'd eat in a valley somewhere and then return to the city late at night, exhausted.

I don't know what Alfonso does on Sundays. Maybe he gets up early and makes himself a cup of coffee, then reads the paper. Or maybe he gets up and asks the maid to get his breakfast, or wakes up once his wife has put it on the table. Maybe he then holes up in his study to work on his research project about water usage in the Valley of Mexico, until his children arrive: family meal time. He could go to the Santa Rosa Market not far from his house to buy the fruits he likes so much, or shellfish for the meal; but more likely he and his family go out to eat at a restaurant known for its fine wines. I can't imagine how he spends his Sunday afternoons or evenings. I don't pry because that's his own and his family's business, and if I knew I'd probably feel hurt, I'd be aware of specific things that we don't share, when there are so many other things that we do enjoy together.

On Sundays I don't think about Alfonso so that I won't miss him; and to keep my mind off him, I make up chores, distract myself. I tend to the plants in my apartment, and while I water the violets I see Grandfather laughing at me:

"Violets, pink; violets, white; violets, blue."

On Sundays I rearrange my closet and do the food shopping for the week. I go out with my girlfriends to eat and then to a movie or a play. Sometimes I leave the city on weekends: there's always somebody with a house in Tepoztlán, in Cuautla, in Atlihuayán. I spend those Sundays in the country relaxing, reading, sunbathing, and forgetting the world. I don't allow myself to think about Alfonso.

I can't get back to sleep. I don't understand what's keeping Alfonso. Maybe he was hungry and decided to go down to breakfast. I get up and pace the room, waiting for him. I turn on the clock-radio. I don't pay much attention to the music: it's just there for company. I look at myself in the mirror and decide to shower. I wish Alfonso were her to rub soap up and down my back.

Ella Fitzgerald's unmistakable voice comes over the radio. I step out of the stall and get dressed.

"It's Sunday," I say. "Thinking about Alfonso is off limits. He'll be back soon."

I look out the window at the docks. The sun is up and the day feels warmer. The plaza begins to come alive, to fill with people, vendors, couples holding hands, mothers hurrying along their freshly bathed, clean children toward San Andrés Church. Waves break on the beach. I don't see Alfonso.

As I finish combing my hair I hear the door open.

"Good morning," Alfonso greets me.

I don't ask him where he's been. He has a right to his own privacy. Ella Fitzgerald sings on the radio:

"It's so nice to have a man around the house..."

"It's Sunday," I tell him as I hug him and cheerfully sing along with the voice that repeats:

"It's so nice to have a man around the house..."

I know that this Sunday is, really and truly, Sunday.

Alfonso smiles, he's holding a flower.

"Rose, red," I tell him, and I kiss the hand that gives it to me.

Translated by Nancy Abraham Hall

NICOLASA AND THE LACEWORK

MÓNICA LAVÍN

"Lace," thought Nicolasa as she formed a set of butterfly wings over the bobbin cushion. "Who decided lessons from grandmothers and great grandmothers should be mandatory, and that lacework must be handed down?"

"This one belonged to your Grandmother Ana," her mother told her, as she pictured her own mother by the balcony, and imagined her hands moving to the rhythm of an ever expanding piece of lace. Women's hours in which threads were drawn over satin cushions, shaping a pine grove, a bit of light in a small patch of sky.

What difference does it make? she asked herself, bored, looking down the street. It was lunch time. She had finished the strip of lace that would trim the pillows of her new bed after the wedding in May. "This will be the last piece of lace I make, and it will be all knotty," she reproached herself as she held her work up to the light. "This butterfly looks like a bull. It'll do." She tucked it in the wardrobe drawer along with other pieces, and went in search of her demi-boots so she could go the plaza and have a cup of chocolate with Angeles.

"You'll have to undo it carefully, if you drop a single thread it's ruined, and mother won't be pleased."

"Be quiet, she might hear you. Good thing she doesn't see that well any more."

"But don't you realize she made this pillow for your wedding?"

With the talented, agile hands she had inherited, Juana traced the stitches made by her mother on the lace border now detached from its pillowcase.

"Mama certainly made tight, small stitches."

"Listen Juana, you're taking too long. Look, have you noticed? There's an N embroidered on the edge. It's so pretty, with its very swirly legs entwined in a garland."

"I've decided we won't use this lace, we'll leave the pillowcase as it is. It's beautiful."

"But Juana..." sighed María, disappointed.

"Not another word. It's very pretty with the initial. Maybe when you get married you can use it for your bed, but you'll have to choose someone named Nero or Nicanor."

They both burst out laughing as Juana folded the altered pillowcase and closed the wardrobe door.

Of the two sisters, Juana, the eldest, married first. The pillowcase with the N on its side and borders of pale lace went to her. For the first time the lace left the house on Pez Street. It left the gallery where Nicolasa rocked away entire afternoons holding her sewing in her hands, and it set out on a journey among other noises. In the web of its design was hidden the squeak of the wooden drawer in which it was kept, and the crinkle of the tissue paper in which it was wrapped, and the low and high taps of Juana and María's footsteps.

The pillowcase was placed, after the honeymoon, on the newlyweds' bed. There, in the afternoon sunlight, the linen began to loose its strong scent of mothballs. The threads of the design became used to the sounds of cars, their motors and horns which rose through the windows, to the swing that came from the gramophone, and the rattling of pots in the kitchen. At night, familiar sounds were repeated: the breathing and sliding of skin. Then there was crying, and small footsteps, and voices became more confused.

One day Juana put the pillowcase away. She folded it between sheets of silk paper and placed it in the bottom of a trunk.

"Only take the small black one," she told the little girl.

With the children bundled in coats, she left the house one morning. Her brother went with her to the station.

"We had to leave the house," she told the little girl as she wiped tears from her small, frightened face. "But we'll be going on a boat. Have you ever seen one? Yes, like the paper ones we used to play with in the park. Only this one will be big, with a swimming pool and a movie theater."

In the dark, they escaped the bomb blasts, traversing level ground, hills, the ocean's edge. Several days later, wearing the same coats and pale complexions, they reached the docked boat.

Hidden in the bottom of the suitcase, the lace, which had

never been anywhere but in the drawer on Pez Street and on a sunlit bed, shook upon the immensity of the Atlantic Ocean.

After one child's prolonged seasickness, a costume party, and a gunshot in one of the staterooms, they landed. In the heat of the new land they undid their coats, and travelled across sugar cane and coffee fields by bus, until they reached a luminous, unknown, and peaceful place.

The lace had changed hands, and with a number of other embroidered items, shawls and mantillas, had been placed in a large, old wooden chest. Comfortably surrounded by the familiar smell of mothballs, it rediscovered the crinkling of the rice paper in which it was stored.

The girl from the boat, who was no longer a child, often looked at the lace when she was alone, and proudly considered it a melancholy proof of origin. She would hold the lace in her hands for a long time, scrutinizing from among the butterflies and the undulating border, a hidden story, as if the weight of the fresh linen in her hands and the minuteness of the tatting were brushing her grandmother's hand, or her mother's head were resting upon it. Overcome, she would quickly tuck it back into its paper bed, and leave it locked in the large chest. The memories were painful, especially when they breathed in her hands.

One day the little girls came down into the living room. It was early and their parents were still asleep.

"Let's open the big chest," proposed the eldest.

As if in search of great treasure, they turned the iron key that was always in the lock. They rummaged through the clothes, the cloth, an old comb and fan decorated with little porcelain faces. At the bottom they found the item wrapped in tissue paper, and they carefully laid it out.

"It's a sack."

"No, it's a pillowcase."

They took it to the window and held it up to the light.

"Look, there's a sky with butterflies!" exclaimed the youngest.

Holding the white linen up high in their hands, they didn't want to let go of it. Without knowing why, they were mesmerized by the softness of the lacy border and the smell of naphthalene burning in the sun.

"There's an N on it, see?"

"An N for *niñas,*" they cried. "It's ours!"

And as they climbed the stairs their bedroom, they spread it out and tried it on several different ways. Convinced that it was useless as a dress-up costume, they cut it down the middle with a pair of scissors, being careful to give each half an equal portion of the letter N. It became a blanket for dolls sleeping in little plastic beds, and lost the smell of naphthalene forever.

Translated by Nancy Abraham Hall

WHITE LIES

ANGELES MASTRETTA

She had unquiet shoulders and a neck of porcelain. Her hair was chestnut brown and unruly, and her quick, merciless tongue could tell all regarding the life and miracles of whoever was under discussion.

Everyone liked talking to her because her voice was like a beacon, and her eyes could turn the most insignificant gestures and obscure stories into clear words.

It wasn't that she made up lies about other people or knew more gossip than anyone else. It was her ability to get to the core of any intrigue, to discover the divine oversight behind a person's ugliness, or to latch onto the verbal miscue that would betray the candid soul.

Aunt Charo enjoyed being involved with the world, checking

it out with her eyes, honing it with her anxious voice. She was not one to waste time. As she spoke, she would sew, embroider her husband's initials on his handkerchiefs, knit vests for anyone who was cold in the winter, play handball with her sister, make the most delicious cornbread cakes, shape *buñuelos* on her knees, and help the children with their homework.

She would never have been ashamed of her passion for words had she not accepted an invitation one afternoon in June to one of those spiritual meetings where the priest spoke on the topic "Thou shalt not bear false witness." At one point, discussing big lies, he noticed that his drowsy listeners remained totally unmoved. So he began to blast away at those tiny venal sins that pop up when talking about other people and which, put together, add up to one big mortal sin.

Aunt Charo left church with a deep sense of remorse in the pit of her stomach. Could it be she was guilty of a mortal sin, the sum of all those times she had talked about this lady's nose and that one's legs, this man's jacket and the hump on so-and-so's back, the guy who struck it rich, and the wandering eyes of such and such a married woman? Could it be that her heart was rotten with sin as a result of knowing everything that went on beneath all the skirts and all the pants in town, knowing all the folly that stood in the way of other people's happiness and all the happiness that was nothing more than folly? These thoughts only increased her fears. Before going home, she stopped for confession with the recently arrived Spanish priest. He was a small gentle man who wandered about the parish in search of faithful souls willing to place their confidence in him.

Now, people in Puebla can love with an intensity that is much greater than in other places, only it takes them time. They don't just latch onto the first stranger who comes along and open up to him as if they had known him all their lives. But in this respect the aunt was not like everyone else in town. She was one of the Spanish priest's first clients. The old priest who had presided over her first communion died leaving her with no one in whom to confide her innermost thoughts, the thoughts that she and her conscience reserved to themselves, the ones dealing with her wayward moments, with her doubts regarding her most private garments, the gurglings of her body, and the dark facets of her heart.

"Hail Mary, full of grace," said the Spanish priest with the terse accent that seemed better suited to a gypsy balladeer than a priest educated in Madrid.

"Who conceived without sin," said the aunt, smiling in the darkness of the confessional, as she did every time she repeated that phrase.

"Are you smiling?" the Spanish priest asked her, guessing that she was as if he were some kind of wizard.

"No, Father," said Aunt Charo, fearing the unpleasant aftertaste of the Inquisition.

"*I* am," said the little man. "And you may, too, with my permission. I can't imagine a more ridiculous greeting. But tell me, how are you? What is it that's troubling you so late in the day?"

"I've been asking myself, Father," said Aunt Charo, "if it's a sin to talk about other people. You know, talk about what's happening to them, find out what they're thinking, disagree with what they say, call the cross-eyed man cross-eyed, the lame woman lame, the skinny guy a slob, and the woman who blabs about her husband's millions snooty. Knowing where the husband got his millions and who else he spends them on. Is that a sin, Father?" asked the aunt.

"No, my dear," said the Spanish priest. "That's called having a thirst for life. What are people around here supposed to do? Just work and say their prayers? That leaves a lot of time in the day. Seeing is no sin, and neither is talking. Go in peace. You have nothing to worry about."

"Thank you, Father," said Aunt Charo, and she ran home quickly to tell it all to her sister.

Free of guilt from that point on, she continued to rejoice in the soap opera the city laid in her lap. Her head was filled with everyone else's comings and goings; it was guaranteed entertainment. That's why she was invited to knit at all the charity bazaars. A dozen women fought to have her at their canasta tables. Those who couldn't see her there invited her over to their houses or stopped by to visit. No one was ever intentionally misled by listening to her, nor was there any new gossip that did not originate with her.

And so life flowed along its course until one evening at the bazaar of Guadalupe. Aunt Charo had spent the afternoon struggling with the beads on a belt, and since she had nothing new to offer, she decided to listen.

"Charo, you know the Spanish priest at the church of San Javier, don't you?" a lady asked her as she was finishing the hem on a napkin.

"Why?" asked Aunt Charo, who did not part easily with information pertaining to herself.

"Because they say he's no priest but a lying Republican who came over with the other exiles that the Cárdenas government took in. And since he couldn't find work as a poet, he made up the story that he was priest and that his papers were burned by the communists along with the church in his village."

"Some people talk too much," said Aunt Charo, then added in her most authoritative manner, "The Spanish priest is devout, a true Catholic. He is incapable of telling a lie. I saw the letter issued by the Vatican that sent him to see the parish priest at San Javier. That the poor old priest was dying just as he arrived wasn't his fault. He didn't have time to give it to him. But as for whether they sent him, of course they sent him. I wouldn't have a faker for a confessor?"

"He's your confessor?" asked one of the curious.

"I'm proud to say he is," said Aunt Charo, keeping her eyes fixed on the beaded flower she was embroidering and putting an end to the conversation right there.

The next morning she went to the Spanish priest's confessional.

"Father, I've told lies," said the aunt.

"Were they white lies?" asked the priest.

"They were necessary lies," answered the aunt.

"Necessary to protect someone?" the priest asked again.

"To protect someone's honor," said the aunt.

"Is the party in question innocent?"

"I don't know, Father," confessed the aunt.

"Then it was a double good deed that you did," said the Spaniard. "May God grant you a clear head and good milk. Go with Him."

"Thank you, Father, " said the aunt.

"Thank *you*," answered the strange priest, which made her tremble.

Translated by John Incledon

NOODLE SOUP

CRISTINA PACHECO

One P.M.: For more than an hour Luz has been shuttling back and forth between the sink and the stove in the corner. When she's not washing dishes, she's checking the burners to see how the food is doing. She takes a sample from the pot, holds it in the palm of her hand, then tastes:

"The soup's just about ready, so you'll have to head out soon," she says to Josefina, the daughter who will go in her place to deliver dinner to Santos.

Since early this morning, when her husband left for work, Luz has worn the baggy, sleeveless dress that hangs in the front as if she were still expecting. But she's not. Her youngest will soon be two months old. His name is Cruz because he was born on the third of May. During the day the baby sleeps in his parents' bed "so that I can keep an eye on him from here, from the kitchen. At night, I switch him to Lety's crib."

When she finishes grinding the salsa, Luz goes back to the stove. She peers into the clay pot and discouraged, says:

"It looks like you'll have to go without the beans. They're hard as rocks. I hate to buy them around here; everything's so stale," she insists, as she places the lunchbox on the table. "You're getting a late start, so take the Metro. Be very careful crossing the street. You remember where to get off, don't you?"

Josefina listens to her in silence, eyes wide, as if trying to memorize everything her mother tells her.

"Your dad is going to be angry when he sees you; he doesn't like you out on the streets alone but at this point, there's no choice. Tell him I got hung up waiting for the man who's coming to fix the gas; it's still leaking even though I plugged the little hole with a chunk of soap. I think I better shut it off as soon as the beans start boiling again, because I'm always afraid, the last thing we need is to be blown up."

Luz stops short when she sees her three sons tripping over one another as they enter the kitchen. The boys' restlessness makes her mad.

"As soon as you smell the soup, you decide to show up, right? Bunch of lousy kids!" Rogelio, the oldest, moves toward the stove, anxious to see what's boiling over the flame. "Out of my way, young man. Can't you see that you could knock over the pot? What are you after? I'm cooking beans."

"Ugh, not beans again..."

"Well, what did you expect, angels' breasts or something?"

Dressed in an undershirt that covers only half her body, Leticia appears. She picks up a toy cup she finds on the floor, raises it and says in baby talk:

"Soup, sou...."

"Soup, my foot. First we send a bowl to your father. You be patient, little lady, we'll eat in a minute." Luz feels boxed in by her children and yells at them. "All of you get out of here and go play somewhere else; you don't have to be right on top of me. Josefina, grab two Metro tickets from my pocketbook. And, for the hundredth time, will you put some underpants on your sister? Just look how she's dressed!"

One twenty-five P.M.: As she walks, Josefina is happy to hear light tap of the lunchbox clasps. She associates the sound with good times: when her father has work, and there's food in the house. At "The Parrots," the small stand where the local wiseguys drink, she crosses the street and walks along the riverbank; that way she avoids being brushed by their hands. Even so, she can't help hearing certain comments that make her blush.

Finally she reaches the subway station. As soon as she steps onto the platform she feels the crush of the crowd pressing toward the car. In a hurry, she doesn't hesitate to jump aboard just as the doors are about to close. "You almost got caught," says an anonymous voice.

The lunchbox rattles with the motion of the train. The aroma of the food is barely detectable among the many odors that permeate the car. Josefina smiles when a harmless drunk standing next to her says, "It sure smells good." Someone makes a comment that has a double meaning. People start to move again as passengers who want to get off crowd around the doorway, oblivious to the folks they hit or shove. Josefina doesn't have time to protect herself from the mob, loses her balance, and in an instant sees a small puddle of noodle soup at her feet.

"Geez, you stained my pants," says a man, stomping.

"Move back a bit, we're being crushed."

"Did you spill the whole thing? All of it?What a shame, I could tell it was delicious," says a little old lady dressed in bright colors.

"And with the price of food these days, spilling it... The worst part is that not even a dog can take advantage of it in here."

One fifty-eight P.M.: Josefina doesn't say a word. She just stares at the soup, which has already begun to look repulsive. She stiffly takes the cover someone hands her: "It landed way over there." Ashamed, the girl can no longer stand the comments, and decides to get off ahead of her stop. On her way to the door she feels herself slip on a greasy puddle.

Josefina is sad. The clink of the empty lunchbox suffocates her. While she considers whether to climb the stairs and board the Metro headed home, she thinks about Lety, about her brothers waiting for dinner to be served, about her mother who had to fend them off so they wouldn't eat their father's portion. Fearful of the severe punishment that awaits her, she is more upset to think that today her father will have nothing to eat.

Far from that spot, near the door of the carpentry shop where he works, Santos looks up and down the street. Over and over he asks himself: "What could have happened? Nobody's brought me any food and it's getting very late."

Translated by Nancy Abraham Hall

THE TURTLE

BRIANDA DOMECQ

Near the beach the sea becomes more transparent. The turgid sun extends a blanket of light over the water; the brilliance disperses and navigates on sparkles of opposing fluctuations; from the depths, blue-green lances pierce the waves, swell, and are lost on the surface. The air grows still and gentle breathing of the sea repeats "ussh - ahhhh" across the long tongue of the white beach. The swaying water deposits a battered coconut on the sand. Little fish sketch a translucent geometry with the reflections from their fins. A little way from shore—just before the breakwater—the sea reverberates and sings.

In the secret fibers of an ancestral memory, the turtle registers the luminous and tepid vibrations, and feeling the resonance in her ample body she follows her dark impulse. She breathes and dives, breaking the mirror of the water with her hard shell, leaving behind her a wake of bubbles, and then emerges. She is near. In the folds of her wide neck, in the softness of her belly, in the fleshy parts of her flippers, she absorbs the messages from the dispararate layers of the sea, some warm, some cool. As she approaches, she scatters the sparkles across the surface. She is all trembling and joy; she is near, she is returning. She finds her own flesh engraved in the darkness, the memory of that other primal darkness, and something in her sings. Bird of the water, kite of the deep sea, she returns with the tug of the tenacious string, and true to instinct she follows just one command: nest.

*   *   *

The man hurries toward the beach, sliding down the side of the dune. He stops. Feeling the sun at its zenith, he shades his eyes with a hand and his glance fans across the sea. The reflection blinds him; his eyes adjust to the brilliance, and then he sees them: small lumps floating on the silky luster of the water. He spins on his heels, returns rapidly to the dune, instinctively following his own footprints, and disappears. The splendor of the day closes over the wound of his presence.

*   *   *

The limitless solitude of the water shines, an extensive and beautiful loneliness. The sea. The consciousness of the breeze and its tributaries that make paths of light, and an agile texture of the sun. The turtle hovers in a strange expectation, floating tranquilly without knowing, without asking, feeling the cycle that is approaching in the fullness of her gut. She is possessed by powerful energy, the same energy that compelled her to break the eggshell and crawl out so tiny that the first race across the beach seemed infinite; dodging dangers, mountains and valleys of sand, the claw of a crab, until she was picked up by the edge of a wave, tumbled about, dragged into the water and sent on her prolonged journey. And now she returns, treading on the almost-forgotten echoes of that beginning and feeling once again the urgency of life, suddenly recognizing her own yearning in another turtle that is swimming nearby.

* * *

In the shelter of the bay the boats rock quietly on the gentle waves. The man arrives, and whistles; the other one hurries to meet him. They speak and their gestures disturb the stillness. They look at the sun, make calculations, nod in agreement, and walk away.

* * *

The beach is calm at midday. The wind urges on the tide, combs the palm trees, and retreats. The sun dominates the landscape; its sparkles collide and reflect each other as they break into bits of color among the grains of sand. The water travels slowly, drawing lacy patterns on the beach. And suddenly a wave swells up and crashes, tumbling into foam and spray, then withdraws. The turtle doesn't wait any more; her nostrils are full of a scent that awakens and paralyzes her. Her companion silently begins a strange aquatic dance, rubbing her shell with his flippers, bumping her gently with his head, in a mute sequence of signals. The dance, the signals, the shoves all make her restless, but they quell her impulse to escape. She is all instinct and need, an ancestral memory that dictates her responses and subdues her fear. She carries inside her a treasure lode of mature eggs, still dormant but eager for life.

* * *

A hungry dog emerges from the bushes, sniffs, and stands still. Across the burning sand the seagulls embroider their intricate discourse. A crab escapes and flees for his life. The dog moves, her droopy teats swinging back and forth as she trots across the sand. The birds fly up with a squawking protest, swoop around in a small arch, then land a short distance away. The dog looks at them; the hunger sits down in her belly and waits.

* * *

In the water, the couple is not in a hurry. The heat of midday, the striking sunlight that makes them open and shut their eyes, and the warmth of the surfacewater lull their movements to a slow sway, a gradual approach. She is still, he is swimming around her, watching her lethargy settle in. Then, a strange movement and she feels the jawbone of the male on her back. Her flippers come alive, but he is already on top of her, holding her still with his strong claws. An awkward revolving of shells stirs up the surrounding water, putting an end to the wait. The female feels the weight of the male, his harsh claws grasping

her back, and she tries to free herself. She struggles to flee to
the tranquility of deep water when suddenly she is overwhelmed
by the unexpected rupture of her solitude and the imminence of
a strange plenitude in which the limits of her own existence are
dissolved. Something is completed, something fulfilled and per-
fected that connects all the facets of her wandering and binds
them together in silence. The restlessness of her secret eggs
seems to swell her insides almost to the point of bursting.
Gently the turtles are rocked by the ample embrace of the sea.

* * *

The breeze diminishes. The great silk-cotton tree extends it6
blanket of heavy shade over the hut. The heat dozes outside.
The dog appears at the door, growls at the puppy that approaches her, and enters furtively, a shadow among shadows, staying
close to the wall. She lies down on the cool floor. Her snout
trembles against the hard earth; two cautious eyes observe. The
man at the table clanks his spoon against the metal plate, sips
the watery soup, stirs and sips, his head down, his eyes fixed.
A transistor radio fills the air with static; a woman's voice sings;
the static returns. The child cries. Crouching before the fire the
woman heats up tortillas. "Shhh, shhh." She hands the tortillas
to the man; she stands and picks up her child, "shhh, shhh."
From the folds of her blouse she pulls her swollen breast, the little mouth attaches to it, the woman crouches down again next
to the fire. In the shadow lies the dog; only her eyes move, from
the woman to the child to the man to the woman. The man nois-
ily pushes his plate away from him, the dog jumps. "Get out!",
and after her retreating tail flies a beer bottle; it rolls and stops
next to a stone, pierced by a sharp ray of sunshine.

* * *

Gradually the sun surrenders its reign. The afternoon breeze pushes rows of white clouds, stirs them up, and forms them again. Over the mountain the pallid pupil of the moon appears, contemplates the landscape for a moment, then blinks shut behind a cloud. The female turtle is slowly convinced of the dance, shell on top of shell, she tilts and rocks to the rhythm of the water. Over and over again they separate and seek each other, they dive and surface, oblivious to time. A pelican glides through the air, dives, emerges, shakes himself, and swallows, taking off from the water once more. The turtle is lost in a millennial memory that has the voice of the sea and the colors of the air, the coming and going of millions of years, the plenitude of closed cycles. Her flesh sings, rejoices, and opens to the registry of storms and calm, vital, vibrant, full of the rhythm of tides. The sky takes on purple and salmon tones, orange, and a tenuous yellow. Across the sea there are paths of color; early shadows tremble with uncertainty; over the mountain a cautious moon dares to show itself.

* * *

The cradle rocks to the rhythm of a distracted hand. With a different rhythm, the other hand combs limp hair, reviving its shine in the light of the fire. The man sits up in the hammock, puts his feet on the floor, takes a knife and stone from the wall. He scrapes, files, prepares. "I want to get there early." The woman gets up, the cradle becomes still; she picks up a bag and prepares a taco with beans and a tortilla. The man snaps his fingers, the dog comes running, and together they start down the path.

*   *   *

The blind eye of the moon opens onto the sea; the waves crash in crystals of light, drawing ephemeral crisscross patterns. The turtle's strange urgency is reborn inside her; the water feels hostile; her desire changes and she rejects the male. Her body is tense with longing for the beach, a pressing need for land. She flaps her flippers and heads toward the swell of the waves, the thundering sound of the reef. The weight of her body rises and is thrust forward with the swirling water; the memory residing in her flesh travels in reverse, toward the beach. An accommodating wave deposits her on the sand. She begins to row laboriously with her flippers, but her shell and flesh are heavy, and the answer to her urgency is awkward and slow.

*   *   *

Against the moon appears the silhouette of the man, and with him, the hungry dog. His hand calms her; his eyes have seen something. It looks like a trunk or driftwood, but it moves, slowly. "Stay!" He kneels in the sand; the dog slumps down.

*   *   *

Along paths of moonlight the turtle progresses with a cumbersome crawl that occupies her whole being, totally committed to leaving behind her medium. She is unusually awkward away from the smooth gliding of water, as she pushes upward toward the highest part of the beach. Behind her she leaves a wide, symmetric trail with her fins: hard, determined paddles that pull along the bulk of her urgency. She stops, breathes with difficulty, and snorts; she starts again, conquering the beach little by little, recognizing its origin in a wordless memory, and hearing the strong echoes of the beginning: nest.

* * *

Eyes watch her from the dune; the dog and her master are lying on the sand, waiting. The turtle is slow. Another shadow approaches and crouches down. The man growls: "I saw her first. She's mine." The shadow straightens up and moves away. In the man's memory, the hut and the child sleep, the woman keeps watch.

* * *

Fatigue seems to have stopped the turtle completely. She rises up on her flippers, lets out a deep sigh, and continues. An obscure, profound recognition of the sand vibrates in her flesh. Something alerts her and she swirls the sand around her, making the first bed. She rests and begins crawling again. It wasn't there. A new sign and the flippers round out her space. Once again she doesn't finish. The secret memory searches and reminisces.

* * *

The dog whines softly; the man looks at the moon. He counts

the beds. Five. "Damn!" He looks at the moon again and gets restless. The shadow of the other man reappears. In his hand, a bag full of eggs. He gives a little laugh. "That one's yours," he says.

"Fuck you!" is the answer.

*   *   *

She is totally focused on the discovery; she dives into the new bed and knows. She feels hurried now, her flippers like sharp shovels gauge out the hole, a perfect cylinder. The sand flies. The turtle's insides are exploding. Something in her is complete, filling her with ownership. She's there now, fulfilled, and her whole existence surrenders to the rhythm of nature.

*   *   *

The man eagerly crawls across the sand, approaching cautiously, spying on the process. The dog behind him sniffs; her nostrils fill with the smell of eggs. The man contemplates the shiny, white spheres, reflections of the moon, balls of light that fall slowly into the shadows. The turtle, absorbed in her own consummation, doesn't perceive them. For her the perfect space is open, the cylinder of the nest, and from the center of her being she slowly closes the cycle.

The man counts, his eyes fixed on the nest that is being filled. But the turtle stops to rest, with many more eggs still inside her. She lays her hard jawbone on the sand, and once more her flesh rejoices and sings.

The dog becomes impatient and barks. The turtle wakes up from her trance, startled; she shakes herself. Her flesh closes, her flippers push at the sand, covering, hiding, protecting the nest. The cycle has been interrupted.

With his fist the man knocks the dog aside; he grabs the shell of the turtle and turns her over. The blade of the knife flashes in the light of the moon.

* * *

Near the highway the men wait, crouching in the shadows. A car approaches, stops, the trunk opens like a giant mouth. The men come forward, they bargain, weaving intricate accounts in the night air. The bags full of eggs are relinquished; extended hands close and return to their pockets.

* * *

In the hut the woman keeps watch. She stirs the fire, then stands at the door; the man returns. She backs up against the wall silently. He enters, throws the coins on the table. "Son of a bitch! He cheated me!" And he lies down. In the light of the fire the woman sadly counts, fingering the coins over and over again, then puts them away.

* * *

Up on the dune, the silhouette of a man slices the sun in two.

Translated by Kay S. García

An Excerpt From
Where Things Fly

Ethel Krauze

Up and down and very slowly, over stones and ditches and torturous dead end streets, toward bottomless piles of garbage, the fully automatic car, polished, hermetic. Our hands grasping the door, the dash; our feet shoved against the floor, our heads about to smash against the windshield. Octavio caresses the back of my neck quickly, barely. Madame Ambassador lectures us about undocumented workers, names of poverty-stricken neighborhoods. We come to a knot of dusty dirt roads, covered with stones.

"O.K., the notebook, quick," Octavio lets loose, and he begins to spout a list. "Walls, roadside inns, rocks and mud, the skeletal remains of a garden, run-down steps, hurry up!"

I'm paralyzed. I don't understand.

"The notebook! Write this down!" he demands, still reeling off a list of everything he sees. "Rivers full of pipes, puddles of shit, a bouquet of dead flowers..."

I wake up. Notebook and pen, I scribble whatever Octavio says on a bunch of papers. I write without taking my eyes off the stones and the dust, without taking my eyes off his eyes looking at the stones and the dust, my own gaze refining and multiplying itself through his. It really is the skeleton of a garden. How did he ever see the little dead bouquet?

No more prescriptions, canons, parameters, statistics and sociological formulas. A strident reality is suddenly at hand. And Octavio gathers it, millimeter by millimeter, drinks it with his eyes, his mouth, his ears, his nose, his hands. He counts the number of dumps, follows the erratic paths of the black streams, discovers the slide improvised by a group of kids at the edge of an abyss, and the whir of the helicopters over the uncultivated hill. He breathes in the rotten air, the drought, the sting of the sun on the red earth, the rancorous noise of poverty. He gets out of the car, feels the walls of the houses, the roofs, the gates, and stands still for a few seconds, sinking into despair or floating, or feeling faint on the inside, he shakes his head and closes his eyes, then lets loose a flood of sentences, a zigzagging litany of blows and flashes of brilliance that capture the border in all of its cancer. I trail him invisibly, shaking, clinging to the notebook.

"Let's talk to some of the poor people, look," says Enriqueta, pointing to a young girl climbing the hill. Her voice is like a barb on a wire.

"She's got enough to deal with," responds Octavio.

"Oh don't be ridiculous. Look, I've got a list of questions all prepared."

"She's pretty and very, very young."

"She was after water, and I can assure you there is no water around her. That's why she's carrying a pail, let's go."

"She's even younger than you are, Juventina, did you notice? Look at her, look at her."

"She's getting away!" yells the woman.

Enriqueta discovers more underprivileged people in the doorway of a shack. They are bustling about trying to put a piece of glass in their window. She drags us over.

Octavio introduces us. He's a journalist, Enriqueta is the distinguished doctor, and I'm their, well, no real need to be specific when it's none of their business. Their daughter? Their student?

They invite us in, offer soft drinks. They tell us about their activities: the daughter works in the *maquiladora*, the son crosses over to the "other side," they've already sent him back three times, but he managed to cross again just last Sunday. They are from Michoacán.

I can no longer stand the heat, and I need a bathroom. I can't believe anyone lives in this place. Enriqueta asks what brand of soft drinks they usually buy, where they shop for clothes, how many times they go into town, what school the children attend. Scribble, scribble. I lunge for the notebook. Octavio signals me, and I let it be.

"What do you most miss about your homeland, ma'am?" Octavio suddenly asks.

"Oh, sir," the woman straightens up, barely smiling, then slowly slumps. "Everything there was green, sir, and I think

maybe that, green things."
I'm watching him, watching him, and smiling.

From there, we head to the wealthy areas. Peninsular highway, sea and sand and the barbed wire slashing between the two countries. Over there blonde children and parks full of trees. Over here rotted, gnarled trunks washed ashore, grimy little colored houses, bruised crowds. The shabby village is a mix of western scenery and hard luck neighborhoods. The rich area consists of barely four or five wood-frame ranch-style houses, and half-baked gardens. Octavio talks, I take notes.

My hair was never messier, my body never so sweaty, sitting by the open car window, wind blasting me, with the ocean as backdrop, the crests of the waves puncturing the bellies of the clouds. Octavio's voice multiplied in each curl, in each stroke, in the hills, at the nape of my neck, in my urge to freeze that moment in time forever.

* * *

We're crossing over to the other side. After long lines at customs, the highway spreads before us. Vast blueness. Spider-shaped pipes: factory smokestacks, up and down bridges and gardens, gardens everywhere.

"Damn!" says Octavio.

"Now you see for yourself," says Enriqueta.

"What a pretty little town... Is it a town?" I say.

I feel I've said something silly, stupid. They know something I don't.

"Aren't you going to dictate anything for me?" I dare ask.

"Open your eyes and ears. For yourself."

I open my eyes so wide I fear they'll pop, and my ears are buzzing. I see skyscrapers, large windows, cleanliness. I hear bells from who knows where. What am I going to write? Octavio said damn; when I said it was pretty, they stopped talking...

"We have no choice," Octavio suddenly says.

"Look," responds the Very Distinguished Doctor with moldy conceit. "You have to keep in mind our parameters, because a sociological approach is something entirely different."

"We simply don't have a choice!"

"Don't be a mechanist, Octavio."

"I see what I see."

What is he seeing? I'd like to write it down.

"That's what I mean, these parameters manifest themselves in the nature of the migratory phenomenon."

"What do I care about parameters, Enriqueta, for Chrissake! I see the filthy dump we just came from and the insolent perfection of these streets and these people. I'm ashamed, I'm overcome by compassion, indignation, and yet I still have the nerve to come here as a reporter.. It's not a barbed wire fence that separates us, look, even the air is different. We're living in different centuries!"

He holds his cigarette so tightly he destroys it. He tosses it out the window. Shake of the head. The eyes, his eyes, is he crying? I don't dare touch him. I've never seen him like this. Is he capable of crying over something like this?

"I'm crying again, Octavio. Are you leaving me? Maybe you're telling me you're leaving, that you've had enough, that you're tired of me, right?"

"I wish I could cry like you."

"Over me?"

"Over everything, everything..."

But I don't understand. Leaving me doesn't hurt him, and this beautiful panorama does? And yet...something very delicate, like a tender anguish overcomes me, and turns me toward him. His wet eyes. The violence of his hands.

Translated by Nancy Abraham Hall

IV.
BEYOND THE GAZE

ABBREVIATED WORLD

ANGELINA MUÑIZ-HUBERMAN

Next to the forest was where the men erected fences of barbed wire and created an abbreviated, enclosed world. They constructed watch towers, and steel-helmeted soldiers with machine guns waited. Inside, they placed naked houses, gray and cold, without chimneys, and with windows lacking panes of glass.

They say that butterflies did not fly there nor did flowers grow, that the sun did not warm nor was the air transparent. Neither were there trees, nor birds which might find a place to nest. The soft bustle of the nearby forest, rubbing of leaf against leaf, little crystalline river, muffled buzzing of winged insects, unique fragrance of variegated flowers, a track which surprises or a discordant sound, verdure of cool shadow, soft bustle, in short, never reached the fenced camp. As if the birds suspended their flight faced with the unknown, as if the water and air kept silent, as if life ended and a cosmic paralysis floated menacingly. No living being crossed that piece of sky. Who can look into the void?

And below, within the limits of that camp fenced by men, a little life began to grow. Children, many children dressed in an unwonted fashion, long dark topcoats down to the ground, pants which drag along, clothing from other bodies which does not find its measure. Mistaken clothing, but desired clothing. Whoever has an overcoat, even if it is stained with blood, will not let it go. Whoever could remove a shirt from a dead person will use it. And the most fortunate of all, the one who managed to get a pair of shoes of any size. Moth-eaten, sweaty, dark and foul-smelling clothing. Clothing, all of it, however, with a symbol: upon the left sleeve, an embroidered yellow star. This is the uniform of the children who fill the gray houses of the camp surrounded by barbed wire and watched over from gray towers by soldiers with high black boots.

The children are numerous and they don't know why they have been taken there. They are hungry and fatigued and the cold at night does not let them sleep. When they understand that they are to spend days or months or perhaps years in that place, they wash their clothes and hang them in the pale sun. Their naked bodies shiver and their bones collide. They have all been shaved and short tufts of hair are beginning to grow. Some perhaps may live until their heads are covered again with hair turned topsy-turvy. Others, perhaps, will not live.

Within the camp there is a spell: nothing shines nor does anything have any color. If the sky is not seen it is because evil black wings cover it. Black wings of a dragon, king of death and desolation.

The dragon which is born again every time that man sins and invokes him is obedient and faithful to the lips which imprison frogs and snakes.

Dragon with green scales which one by one, a thousand by a thousand, mesh perfectly and go from more to less and from less to more, molding the imposing body, the extremely long wings, the cruel tail and the legs ending in powerful claws. His head, if not so ferocious in repose, with the jaws opened, shoots flames to right and left without pity. A dragon which we believed existed only in fairy tales and because of our error was born again.

Thus it is that the man who invokes the dragon becomes his slave and has to feed the swollen belly and its insatiable appetite. Because the dragon promises him everything but demands everything of him.

The dragon continues contaminating slowly with his lethal fire and the men who adore him mark their bodies in front of him and spill drops of blood like an auspicious sacrifice. These men, with the engraved sign of dragon fire, are no longer free, they are the sword which gradually penetrates the bodies of men who are still free. They aspire to total power in the world and make the asphyxiating branches and poisonous herbs grow. The dragon reigns in the heart of these men and their eyes no longer see, nor does their skin feel, nor their ears hear; but, on the other hand, their pulse is an infallible dart, their strength, a weighty chain, their muscles, appliances of steel.

They manufacture powerful weapons and torture those who do not convert to their madness. The dragon knows how to implant in them drops of blindness and lightning bolts of hatred. At their passing, they destroy and trample and spit on everything.

They have sworn to kill all the children who wear the yellow star. They bring them from all the corners of the earth and wait until the time of death arrives.

The dragon also, from high above, cheerfully awaits the tender food which he is to receive, extends his wings and darkens each day even more.

The darkness is such that one can barely distinguish the cycle of the sun from the moon. It is getting colder and the children join together, body to body, to gather some bit of heat. They take each other by the hand and sing and begin to dance, a slow dance and an unintelligible song. Children are like that.

The dragon becomes disturbed and beats its wings. Its glittering scales fall like small splinters of glass in a fine rain. Such is the dragon.

But the soldiers are not like that and they clutch their weapons and redouble their vigilance. They polish their high boots and make their guns gleam.

It happens that one day the children begin to draw, and everything that was missing in that narrow, enclosed world begins appearing on scraps of paper gathered from any corner. Red suns, houses with doors and windows with cheery curtains, smoking chimneys and roads bordered with flowers which lead to the house and tall trees in the background. Boys and girls who jump and play; even dogs and cats and birds and butterflies, especially butterflies. Great blue flowers stuck on the walls. Sunlight overflowing everywhere.

But this is not tolerated. It is not possible to create light in a dark world. A smile is not permitted. The dragon brings total blackness. The soldiers take the children out one by one. One by

one they are raised in fire towards the jaws of the dragon.
And yet higher and higher still, until they reach the open sky.

Wrapped in flames, their bodies gleam and illuminate. The intensity of the light is such that the soldiers and the vanquished dragon are blinded, but not before they are able to contemplate, in astonishment, a new enclosed paradise where the multicolored butterflies of fire are so numerous that the children will not be able to catch them.

Translated by Roberta Gordenstein

STATE OF SIEGE

ELENA PONIATOWSKA

I walk along the main avenues, the wide black surfaces, the sidewalks on which everyone fits and no one sees me; no one turns around, no one looks at me, not a single one of them. Not one person shows the least sign of recognition. I insist. Love me. Help me. Yes, everyone. You. I see you all. I try to magnetically draw them towards me; nothing retains them, their gazes slide over me, erase me, I am invisible. Their eyes avoid resting on any one thing, and I look at them all so intently, I imprint them on my soul, on my forehead; their faces bore into me, they accompany me; I imagine them, I recreate them, I caress them. We women treasure faces; in fact at any given moment life becomes a single face that we can touch with our lips. Love me, see me, here I am. I put all life's forces on alert; I want to pass through the panes of the box-office window and say, "*Señora, señora,* it's me," but nobody, nobody turns their head, I am as smooth as the opposite wall. I should yell at them, "Your community would be incomplete without me, no one walks like me, no one has my laugh, my way of wrinkling my nose when I smile, you'll never see a woman rest her elbows on the table the way I do, no one buries her face in her shoulder...ladies, gentlemen, children, dogs, cats, inhabitants of the entire world, believe me, it's true, you need me."

I would like to think that they hear me, but I know it's not true. No one waits for me. Nevertheless, every day, stubbornly, I take to the road, I go out onto the wide avenues, to that great intimate desert so like the one I have inside me. I need to touch it, see with my eyes what I have lost, I need to look at that black extension of tar, I need to see my death.

Translated by Nancy Abraham Hall

The Guardian Angel

Guadalupe Dueñas

Since childhood I have known that everybody has a guardian angel, an angel in whose custody life is lived. Yes, don't smile, I saw him next to my cradle; then in dreams, and on numerous occasions, I perceived the brush of his wings. Once I saw his back as he walked away from me, even though a celestial being created to serve me exclusively would never walk out. At times he was a golden adolescent like an altarpiece, at times a sensation, a trace of moss, an echo. I insist that when he was near, darkness lost its meaning and fear was only a vague memory. Later he dissolved into time.

Yesterday he appeared again, now that I no longer believe in illusions nor recall my childish ways: setting aside a special place for him on my pillow so he could keep watch while I slept, invoking his protection with every mother's invariable prayer:

"My Holy Guardian Angel, sweet companion, do not desert me by night or by day," a refrain I have repeated all my life without pondering its meaning.

I have seen him again, as real as in the beginning, when the end seemed so remote. The same face, the same attitude, although now there is a certain mystery about him: I can barely distinguish his plumage, his brilliance and soft shadow are shrouded in mist. Perhaps he is within arm's reach, perhaps I could caress him like a small mocking bird; I'd like to touch his heart and dry my last tear by his luminescent candle, but I don't dare try. I let him float like August clouds, so blue they turn violet and gradually break up, becoming liquid and pale as the wind. I no longer know whether it is true that one day he fled my wailing. Oh, my Job-like complaints required the dike of his wings! Where was he when loneliness grew like a tornado, and everything in the world was beautiful except love? Love, no, not that! For me it was always out of reach, an infinite number of light years away. He had to know it. As my guardian he saw me howl like a wolf running to and fro on the heels of dementia. He knows all my ghosts, his subtle fingers touched my scars. Unnameable insanities, crazy projects, miserable shreds of absurd pages are hidden in his saddlebags. At first, a splendid dawn, delightful trees, sea, and fruit. Then a landscape of sand and roaring wind. Following the delirium, a funeral song. For every dream, devastation; for the dawn, a requiem; for the water, a prayer for the dead.

Messenger of God, you were never like the angel I heard about in school, the one who stops a girl from leaping into the void as his silken curls, like golden butterflies, caress the nearby rocks. And you're not like the picture in the book, appearing at the precise instant in which the serpent releases its venom. In another picture you proceed down a path with a blonde boy, coming between him and a young girl with passion in her eyes. Sublime Angel of Mine! My longing to fuse with He who remains and endures for eternity was frozen in your nomadic journey through life. There was no reclamation nor fiery sign: only a rope broke my precipitous fall, hidden seal of the Chosen One, second Adam, he who redeems me and is known to you.

Celestial Spirit, what were you doing when I was walking blindly through a storm of nails? When I was thirsty I did not hear you murmur, and when waves washed out my path, I did not see the shadow of your Book of Psalms. I was alone in the fog, alone with an uncertain future. I was a small, insatiable hand on a clock, dry to the bone at last. I am nothing, a shadow that leaves and does not return...Loyal Guardian, in what corner of my childhood did I loose you? Where did you go with your lucky halo? Now that I touch eternity today, now that I walk irremissibly today, I see you at last on the opposite bank. Guardian Angel, come with me!

Translated by Nancy Abraham Hall

YOUNG MOTHER

MARÍA LUISA PUGA

Childbirth? No, the delivery was fine, that is, it seemed normal. Of course since it was my first time, I was frightened, but I had spoken to a lot of people, my mother, my friends, even the nurses. It was normal. You think you won't be able to stand it. That you're going to break. That no one realizes, or worse, no one is going to believe you. I think I spent the whole time trying to find a way to tell them that I really couldn't take it any more. I wanted to be sure I had convinced them before I began to scream, to really scream, I mean, because I felt like I was screaming all the time, or moaning, I don't know, but when suddenly someone said all right, you've been very brave, and I heard her—I heard her cry—it was incredible, I was scared, I thought that they had brought her in from the room next door. She cried as if they had shaken her awake. I didn't understand.

I started to cry as well, because I felt very sad and alone, because I knew that they weren't going to understand me. Everyone moved around a lot and I felt that they stretched me, and cleaned me, and applied things to me, and when a nurse told me all right, it's fine, calm down, it's a girl, don't cry, I didn't believe her, I didn't believe it. I thought I had died and was already dreaming—or seeing my life as a dead person. Then I didn't know what happened. When I awoke they brought her to me swaddled and clean so that I could feed her. I did whatever they told me. I felt very clumsy, and could feel her sucking my breast. It was true. Milk came out and something there was sucking it in. I touched her, felt her breathe, but no, I didn't believe it. Then they would take her away, and I would drop into a dark and narrow sleep, like I had during all those months before she was born. A domed space. It's not that it seemed bad to me, I mean, I wasn't scared and nothing hurt me. It was merely the anguish of being on the other side. I don't know when it started. One day I noticed it. Perhaps the first time I felt it. It was very strange. Neither pleasant nor unpleasant. Strange. As if I were two people, but I didn't know the other one. And I began to spy on her. Both were inside my body—no, I'm not talking about the baby. When I thought about the baby it was in a different way. I spoke to her a lot, all the time, I think. And with Mario we planned how things would be after she arrived. But that's a different matter. That was when I made myself not feel the dome, that other presence, that lack of a body. I forced myself, because no one realized anything. Neither Mario nor my mother. Because it wasn't apparent when I looked at myself in the mirror. Because the doctor said that my pregnancy was going well, that my health was good. And if I told him that I felt strange, he would tell me that's normal, it's your first. And I forced myself to believe him. But I dragged that body with me, feeling more and more panic. Feeling that my voice was being pushed further and further down. That only I could hear it. That only by shouting loudly would others hear me. Something in my head was shutting down and growing dark, and I had to move forward in search of another way out, an exit, any exit. From where I was nothing could be seen. Nights began to scare me. When the streets would quiet down, when Mario would shut off the light so we could go to sleep, I became terrified. And in the morning I would watch myself get breakfast, go shopping, prepare the baby's clothing, talk to people knowing that it wasn't true, that it wasn't true, that I wasn't there, but rather trapped in that dome that never ended, that continued, continued, continued and I even tried to get used to it because it people seemed to accept me that way. Mario still loved me and the doctor said everything was wonderful. Sometimes my legs would swell, I felt nauseous, tired, things that happen during pregnancy. I felt so relieved. Those were the only times at which my body and I were the same. And I would talk about my baby. I knew she was there, alive. I felt that I should protect her against that other thing. But I am young, I am strong. That uneasiness didn't last long. It soon disappeared and left only a taste of darkness in my mouth. I knew right away that I was back. Far from everything again. Lost again. I didn't realize that I was becoming increasingly sad. That when I smiled I felt someone else's look on my face. That my laugh was not my own. And I think I didn't realize it because I was hopeful. Or they were hopeful for me, I don't know. Maybe it wasn't even hopefulness. Every time I said I felt depressed they told me it was normal, that it would all be over when the baby was born. That it was due to a shortage of energy and who knows how many other things. That I shouldn't worry. And I began to count the days. To live with my eyes fixed on my due date. to hope out loud. to close my eyes each time I felt the dome. And I think that's why I began to hide it. To pretend whenever I was with someone. Even when I looked in the mirror. It was an effort to breathe. Not much longer, not much longer. When I leave here there will be people outside. I needed to believe that because I needed to believe that there was an end, a door to the other side. And I almost felt curious to see up close what was happening to me. That being there without being there. That not being. That dark sleep. Because I yearned for the other. And my impatience prevented sleep. And when they brought me to the hospital, I clung to the nurses' hands so that they wouldn't leave me there, so that they would drag me to this side, no matter what it took. During labor I saw it clearly. Pain I don't know. Pain was everything. It was being there surrounded by so many people, and I was trapped and alone, not knowing what to do or how to do it. And seeing my baby born, and that she was a girl as I had hoped. Then hearing Mario say yes, she would be called Alina, that she was our baby, that she would show us how to live with her. To feel that she had come from me, to live, and know that no, she hadn't come from beneath the dome, that couldn't be, no one understood me when I said I wasn't well, to hear the new sentence, another of those far off and useless sentences, another illusory label, postnatal depression, it's normal, it lasts a few days, and the scream that took shape within me, that couldn't get out, and my baby who didn't know, trusting, alone like me, alone.

What made me jump? That. The open window in the

bathroom, the bustle of the nurses in the room, the noise of the cars below, the thought of the days and the days and the days. The sky was gray, it was a lead gray square from the window. I didn't look down. We were alone. I jumped.

"And now?"

"When the dome burst I felt strong. Everything is in pieces around me. Alina died. I am broken. Now I'll live as I can, from where I can, with whatever I can."

(From the *Guardian*, London, Dec. 28, 1977:

A young mother suffering from postnatal depression jumped from a fourth floor window at a teaching hospital in London with her three day old baby. The little girl died; the mother, seriously injured, is alive)...

Translated by Nancy Abraham Hall

BIRTHDAY

MARTHA CERDA

That day Papa found a way to desecrate Mama's grave. It was three o'clock in the afternoon and the cemetery was full of visitors carrying flowers to their respective dearly departed. Papa arrived on time for his date with Martha, his secretary, who was waiting for him at the "Cafe Across the Street." The family members placed their flowers in urns set at each headstone for that purpose. "For that purpose," dictated Papa to Martha, the secretary, who attentively followed Papa's words, Papa's gestures, Papa's glances. Papa recalled that it was Mama's birthday, although it had been quite some time since Mama had last fulfilled her duty, and he winked. Martha transcribed the wink in shorthand. Between dots and dashes it was soon five o'clock. The visitors began to leave; Mama's headstone, encircled by many others, was the only one without flowers. Papa encircled

Martha's waist with his arm, and she encircled his leg with hers.
The guards locked the cemetery gate and Papa had to stay in a
hotel room, with Martha.

The next day, at dawn, Mama's grave was open and her skeleton was by the entrance. The guards declared the graveyard's
security system so effective that no one could get in. Or out.

Translated by Nancy Abraham Hall

BEYOND THE GAZE

ALINE PETTERSSON

I t took two people to help her out of the church. She was agitated, shaken. Águeda barely managed to reach the exit, barely managed to reach her own front door.

"It's a dizzy spell. It's nothing, I'll be fine soon."

But her pale, twitching face made her companions doubt. Águeda refused to let them in to make her a cup of tea.

"Don't worry, I'll be good as new once I've rested. Thank you. Thank you."

There was no way to change her mind. The woman shut the door on the people, the day. Águeda was anxious to be alone.

Eyes closed, his face sails through your innermost being, through your rushing blood. His torch-like proximity undoes your virginal refuge, the wall of ice behind which you used to shelter yourself, playing a diffuse and nameless waiting game. But the game has an outcome: Gabriel. There are no words to explain it, to explain the fire that jolts you, that wears down the dike, that gradually allows access to a torrent of moisture. Your skin is a bough of stars, the sea tossed by the moon, rock split by a quake.

Several years had passed since Águeda had arrived on her way through town and her stopover had lengthened until it became a final destination. By then her fame had spread beyond the village limits. Águeda was sought by men, women, old people and children holding their parent's hand. Águeda was the local celebrity. No, not a celebrity, a savior, the voice that was able to summon divine help. The voice that connected her neighbors, their needs, her neighbors' pain to the kingdom beyond. The devotion with which she prayed, even the gestures that accompanied her supplications were a clear sign of her closeness to God. Because Águeda had visions. At first they hadn't believed her. It's not easy to accept that there is a person with exceptional qualities in your midst. But the villagers came to trust in her.

You must submit to the gust that awakens your instincts, that imprisons your modesty, that has turned you into a bonfire lying in wait for the flow that will satiate it. The urgency to approach the knowledge you observe, desire beyond reason and good sense, has descended upon you. You are a temple, altar to that nameless urge that fills you to the brim, and drives you through the vast journey of the flesh. Covered by Gabriel's presence, you reach the highest peaks, trembling woman turned sacrifice.

Little by little Águeda had learned to cure the sick, and received cash as often as a fat hen, some eggs or a basket of fruit or vegetables for her services. In the room where she mainly worked, to the side of the bed, a table always covered by a perfectly starched cloth embroidered with religious motifs. On the table, two clay receptacles held flowers, handfuls of various herbs and a few perpetual candles. Above the table, like a crown, a framed colored print displaying the image of a blonde Christ gazing towards Heaven, arms extended forward in a sweet summons.

When Águeda was accepted by the villagers, when she was no longer considered an outsider, when her cures and supplications proved valid, her mouth began to spout mysterious pronouncements, warnings, calls to heed the dangers of sin that enslaves mankind in such a terrible way, now that there is no time left, and the end of the world is at hand, the air filled with signs.

Your body is an hourglass in which time falls like sand and in each of its grains you would like to sense eternity. Embark on a long trip that takes you to impossible limits, to a melding of light and shadow, to the trembling movement of life that throws itself into the intense rattle of death. Full of rain, each of your crevices, each one of them is an eye that appropriates that ineffable knowledge that lays awake before you, in you, inside you.

Despite the heat, Águeda wore dark clothing, as if in mourning. While the rest of the women bared their arms, hers were always covered, and her shawl rarely slid from her head to rest only on her shoulders. Perhaps that was why it was difficult to know how old she was. No, it wasn't that she was old, it's that time seemed to have taken refuge in her, in a face and a body oblivious to all the years she had spent on Earth. And there wasn't a man whose eyes could view her with anything but respect or reverence.

Águeda had become a major figure. She had even introduced a custom to the monotonous life of the village. On Friday evenings, people gathered at her house. After saying the rosary, which she led with arms raised in the shape of the cross, in a voice nearly broken by spasms, Águeda talked to them about how the world would end soon, and the perfidies of the devil. Once, horrified, she told them how she had been permitted to see the filth of Satan who had spewed semen over the chalice at the moment of consecration. No one from the village received communion the following Sunday. Even Father Juan himself held back, not totally devoid of reverent curiosity. Because she performed enough cures to count on two hands, and the people's devotion and attendance at church had increased so. Words of warning, exhortations to follow the path of righteousness sprouted from Águeda's lips now that time was running out.

Transported in his arms you scale the heights. With your eyes closed you see more than you ever have. You see the sky that opens fold by fold, and you see it's fullness. You feel that you are coming apart, that you are a bottomless crevice that burns like the bush. You feel and die from so much sensation. He opens each of the doors of revelation for you, guides you along unknown paths that surrender to you, as you have surrendered to the fair-haired guide with the moss-like gaze. And you see and listen and you are possessed by the thirst for knowledge.

Little was known about Águeda's life before she came to the village. And no one dared to inquire. In her case it would have been almost a sacrilege, and behind her back they feared that if she ever heard anything, she would leave town. At first, before she settled in, they often saw her gaze lost in the distance; but even back then no one dared ask. Each person carries his or her own pack of troubles. Each person is the sole owner of yesterday's memories. And thus, Águeda settled into the role of a passing pilgrim.

It was after someone had unwittingly heard her scream, that Águeda began to talk about her visions, to alert people about the impending end of time, about the devil that boldly wages his final battles. Yes, behind the partially drawn curtains someone thought he had seen Águeda trembling on the floor, panting, her eyes fixed on the green gaze of the picture, while her hands traveled along her body as if they belonged to someone else, until the rasping cry passed through her lips. But the person who surprised her doubted the vision, and said nothing. Nevertheless, from that point on, her cry was the prelude to new admonitions, after the ecstasy punishment would be unleashed, horrors that only she could see.

You don't want to leave that placeless spot, where your feelings faint as you are penetrated. You dissolve in an ardor whose flames do not burn you. And you look beyond the gaze and hear registers that the limitations of your ear had denied you. You skirt the boundaries of a knowledge for which you have no words. Time is the same, yet other, happening since always and forever. Your body is space and vehicle. In your center orchids have opened and await the rain. They await the rays of sun that lavishly extend and traverse the liquid paths of your skin. You no longer want to see.

Any bit of news runs through a town like wildfire. Facts are so scarce that they supersede life's rituals. Ears crave stories to break the cadences that take man from a cradle of pine until he is deposited in that other pine container, the casket. Any bit of news becomes an event. There was speculation about what had motivated Águeda to come to the village. Someone said she was running away from something, but no one was able to say from what. And thus the years passed, until Sunday's Mass, when the presence of a stranger with green eyes seemed to break the placid weekly routine. And a "What are you doing here, Gabriel?" was heard, and it made the woman lose her strict composure. It took two people to help her to her house. She stayed there alone and did not accept her neighbor's expressions of concern.

Translated by Nancy Abraham Hall

THE SWALLOWS
OF CUERNAVACA

ANGELINA MUÑIZ-HUBERMAN

D avid, now old, had never stopped to think about the swallows. At least not much. Except last summer. When the need to remember had returned to him more imperatively. When he knew he was at the end of the road and death was approaching him with a sure, precise step. When he was left alone.

David's house is small, white with red roof-tiles. The garden is spacious with a few azaleas in distinct shades of rose and lilac and a millennial fig-tree in the center. A fig-tree with branches so dense that beneath its shade not even a blade of grass can grow, but among its branches it shelters, on the other hand, birds in search of a nest and reposing bats. Where the silence of the day is changed into the tumult of the twilight at the return of the birds and the awakening of slow-flying mammals.

David, even with his eyes closed, can tell what moment it is. He has integrated every one of his senses into the life of the house and garden. Sounds. Smells. Light. Touch. Desires. Since he has been alone he no longer views his environment carelessly. Every object, every stroke of life has acquired a space, a time: pilgrims. He wanders through the rooms of the house: he lingers in each one of them: he observes the pieces of furniture: he thinks about changing their position. He observes the bookcase: one by one he reads the titles of the books again: the beloved books: his true belongings: what he most appreciates: to whom will he leave them when he dies?

Then he goes out to the garden. He delights in each patch of earth, in each trail of insect, of nervous ant, of snail, of butterfly flight in the transparent air. He sits down on a bench to enjoy the early-rising sun of Cuernavaca. That sun which warms sufficiently to be grateful to it, to console oneself with it, to be prized company.

And thus, half asleep, he remembers. He remembers his childhood in Seville. Images of places which appear to him with clarity: the mosaic patios and the big vases of wallflowers. The light in the streets: the chiaroscuro of the plazas. The sound of the bells: of the town criers in the dawn. The trotting of the mules with jugs of milk for breakfast. The rolls and the sweets of every flavor. What has disappeared and only remains in his memory: what good does it do to go over and over it?

Why does the mind keep so much space for memories? Who is it going to benefit the day he dies? If he had written it or if he had told it in time. He could have written and he could have told.

Perhaps it is too late. Would it be worthwhile trying?

Perhaps begin the recounting of his days. If he had the strength. If he had the will. As for writing, he had always done that. It was a habit he had not lost. Even if it were only to fill the drawers of his desk with papers. And to put them in order now: before dying.

Now that his days are long he can stretch them to write his memoirs. Because he had lived a long time: almost three centuries: with luck: born at the end of the nineteenth century: lived in the twentieth century: died in the twenty-first century?

The whole story was up to him. He can choose what event to describe: Halley's comet? The First World War? The Spanish Civil War? The Second World War? All the wars that follow?

His life has taken place from one war to another. Now, in Cuernavaca, ex-combatants of other wars sit down in his garden to exchange soliloquies. Also the gardener, when he goes there, talks about Zapata and the Revolution.

David recognizes his story among the stories of the rest. Memory is meant to be transmitted. No one wants to silence what he has seen; what he has lived; the course of the past moves the present. For David and his friends the meaning of continuity is the meaning of the narrative.

With Alan, member of the Lincoln Brigade, he compares fragments of battles, days freed from the calendar, parabolic trajectories of projectiles. Strange events of people who escape death and people who find it. The message not deciphered. The password not heard. The cold and dampness in the trenches. The imminent noise of the bombing. The body trembling to the rhythm of the machine gun. The jerk of the shoulder at the firing of the weapon.

Almost at the same time David and Alan intend to write their memoirs. Both had written in a little writing pad notes of the deeds of war and both preserved details important to communicate. So many years have passed that the moment of calm perspective and renewed remembering of old age has finally arrived.

But David, now that he has been left alone, feels the presence of death closer than ever. He does not know if he will embark upon his work: if his desire and will will be sufficient; if one more testimony will matter.

David, at night, with his bed half-empty, turns over and over without being able to sleep. He still respects the half of the bed which belonged to Laila as if because of that she would return. As if hope needed a void to fill to overflowing. As if habit were a certain kind of palliative. Laila would return; some day she would return.

Why had she left? When did the break occur without him realizing? What blindness, that of one who refuses to see: two lives, one next to the other, never united; always parallel; and now in opposite directions. He did not even know where to look for her. He would not even attempt it.

They had gone through the bombing of Madrid together; all the dangers, all the escapes, all the betrayals; except the last one. In the last one, he remained alone.

He remembered her as a young woman; and he preferred to preserve those years and not the last one. With the meetings at the Cafe de Oriente, or at the Pombo, or at the Happy Whale.

Seated on the bench in the garden of the house in Cuernavaca he mixes his memories, shuffles them, moves them around like dominoes. Which one will appear at this moment? The arrival in Mexico in 1939; and from then on a new life. And finally, what was the ultimate dream: a house in Cuernavaca.

But the ultimate dream was not a house in Cuernavaca; the void had not been filled; memories were the means of inter-weaving and entertaining a story which was finished. He no longer thinks about uselessness or failure; it is the end, in front of his own doors.

What had he left in the end? Two novels in Spain that no one remembered. A book of poems he had just finished. And his memoirs; if he was indeed writing them.

But he did not worry; that had been the course of his life.

Nothing would change it.

He did not mourn.

Events lost everywhere; never the act of cataloging.

When Primitivo the gardener appears, it is to sit down at his side on the bench in the garden and tell his fantastic stories of Emiliano Zapata and his white horse. The white horse which had ascended to heaven at the death of its master and whose tail was waving among the brilliant stars of the sky above Cuernavaca. Orion converted into Emiliano and his horse trot-ting along the Milky Way. Primitivo was even willing to remain until night to show David the living stars.

Between the two, they assemble and disassemble what has not been lived, what will never happen. They turn aside their eyes from the earth which gives pain and laugh at the trans-formed stars. Then Primitivo takes out a bottle of rum and little by little the separation is greater: now they fly through the air without weight or worry.

When Alan arrives the merrymaking increases and among the three they begin a new book of absurd and grotesque thoughts. On sheets of paper they continue writing, with vacillating letter, any word which occurs to them. And the next one, between guffaws, emends it, attaches another meaning to it, scratches it out, erases it. Sprinkles it with rum. Spits on it. Urinates on it. And sets it on fire. They have a good time.

When the sun sets, they leave and David remains a while longer in the garden. Then he enters the house. He is dizzy and only feels like throwing himself on the bed. But first, in a kind of ritual, he opens the drawer of the night table, and reviews carefully what he keeps there: he entertains himself with the pistol: he caresses it: he moves it from one hand to the other: he rests it on its side, on his temple to feel the cold: he takes comfort: he replaces it in the drawer: it's a good thing to know that it is in its place: he can always fall back on it. He lets himself fall backwards on the bed: the alcohol-induced lethargy will make him fall into a deep sleep. Everything will be erased around him and he will not awaken until the morning of the next day is well advanced. With his bed half-empty.

David remembers that it must already be the season when the swallows nest. The same summer that Laila left, a pair of swallows arrived to build its nest under the eaves of the living room window. And the same pair returns every year.

Soon the pair of swallows will arrive.

Soon he will settle down in the rocking chair to observe them for days without end.

How they build their nest.
How they carry the clay.
How they slowly paste it onto the wall.
How they choose the blades of grass and the dry twigs.
The chirping of satisfaction.
Sometimes the discussion over an error committed.
Sometimes the appeal to the observer.
Sometimes the question for approval.
Do you like our little nest, David? Does it seem cozy to you?

David is the swallows' friend, and they are his. They tell each other stories: the swallows know many stories: they travel high through the heavens but their sight hangs onto the earth.

David's memory soars on contemplating the swallows. How has he reached this state of beatitude if his life meant never learning and always choosing the wrong moment: the lie attracted: the lie for the sake of fiction: the dark act at the center.

The truth is that he never fought in the Civil War; he invented his fighting to have something to tell his friends: he fled to France as soon as the war began and there he collected stories from the newspapers and put together his own. In the end he believed it, just like when he was a child he said that ants urinated in his shoes at night. David could describe each battle and his details were exact: even more than if he had been in them: his vision was that of one who had read it all. As for the diary which he pretended to have carried, it was also a betrayal: he certainly did write a diary: but with the tales of soldiers who died and he kept it as if it were his. Some day it would be his and he would be able to repeat it to the others. It was his now and the others already believed it.

Now he could begin to write his memoirs with all those tales which he had appropriated. As soon as the swallows arrived this summer he would be ready. Laila would not be able to accuse him of falsifying.

Besides, the pistol that he guarded jealously was the weapon that he never grasped: a sign of his equivocation: a consolation, if it became necessary: the last exit, in case.

He patiently awaits the arrival of the swallows. One day after another. In the beginning he does not realize that time is advancing. Primitivo and Alan erase it with bottles of rum. David wonders if their stories are not invented like his. (No, his are real: they happened.) Primitivo and Emiliano Zapata's horse. Alan and the battle of the Ebro. David: with the true story in his head. Only the others lie.

He patiently awaits the arrival of the swallows.

But the swallows do not arrive.

If they do not arrive, how will he be able to write his memoirs: his only tale for the others: the justification for the invention of his life: the proof that he is real

David touches himself: it seems to him that he is alive; he still feels. But it is also possible that he might be dead. That Laila has abandoned him may be due to the fact that he is dead. That she considers him dead. That she no longer believes his stories. That his stories are boring. That he has repeated himself too much.

And the swallows continue not to come.

If they do not come, it means, in fact, that he is dead.

They had become aware of it.

A clean shot: in the temple.

The swallows of Cuernavaca do not arrive at David's little house.

Translated by Roberta Gordenstein

A CONCEALING NAKEDNESS

NEDDA G. DE ANHALT

For Virgilio Piñero, i. m.

I am sleeping in the bedroom of a castle. The room is sumptuous; the sheets are of pure silk and I am laying on them, naked. Suddenly I hear a noise. It seems to come from the western side of the large windows. I cover myself with the black velvet spread that I quickly take from the Louis XIV armchair. But the noise is not coming from there, for I clearly hear the key turn, the door creak open, and footsteps approach.

Before me is a strange being, naked.

"What are you looking for?" I ask him.

He doesn't answer right away, but gestures obscenely. Then

he exclaims in a slow, deep voice, "And afterwards I plan to kill you."

"How?" I ask, trying to speak in a serene, even mocking tone.

The gesture he then makes with his hands leaves me frozen with terror. Impulsively I throw the spread over him. The surprise paralyzes him only for an instant; then he tries to free himself, and is about to do so, but I manage to grab the four corners of the spread and pull them together with all my might.

The being convulses as I breathe heavily from exertion. I realize he needs air; I do, too, but if I withdraw I am lost. With great difficulty and as he struggles, I manage to drag him to the fireplace. I throw him on the fire, hitting him mercilessly and incessantly with the poker. The velvet of the spread starts to smoke, and in certain spots it develops reddish brown stains.

The fire dies down and the room fills with smoke. The being, still almost totally covered by the singed blanket, has finally stopped groaning. My naked body perspires. The air is governed by heat and silence.

Trembling I lie back down on the bed and try to cover myself with the sheets. I am exhausted. I am overcome by sleep.

The cold of the dawn and a peculiar odor wake me. I am afraid. I don't want to look toward the fireplace. I press a button on my night table, which one I don't know, the valet, the chambermaid, who knows?

I hear the key turn, the door creak open, and footsteps approach. I cover my nakedness with the sheet, but this time I look straight toward the fireplace. The body's nakedness is revealing. I smile.

Translated by Nancy Abraham Hall

THE SECRET WEAVERS SERIES
Series Editor: Marjorie Agosín

Dedicated to bringing the rich and varied writing by Latin American women to the English-speaking audience.

Volume 11
A NECKLACE OF WORDS
Short Fiction by Mexican Women
152 PAGES $14.00

Volume 10
THE LOST CHRONICLES OF TERRA FIRMA
A Novel by Rosario Aguilar
192 pages $13.00

Volume 9
WHAT IS SECRET
Stories by Chilean Women
304 pages $17.00

Volume 8
HAPPY DAYS, UNCLE SERGIO
A Novel by Magali García Ramis
Translated by Carmen C. Esteves
160 pages $12.00

Volume 7
THESE ARE NOT SWEET GIRLS
Poetry by Latin American Women
368 pages $17.00

Volume 6
PLEASURE IN THE WORD
Erotic Fiction by Latin American Women
Edited by Margarite Fernández Olmos & Lizabeth Paravisini-Gebert
240 pages $19.95 cloth

Volume 5
A GABRIELA MISTRAL READER
Translated by Maria Giacchetti
232 pages $15.00

Volume 3
LANDSCAPES OF A NEW LAND
Short Fiction by Latin American Women
194 pages $12.00

Volume 1
ALFONSINA STORNI: SELECTED POEMS
Edited by Marion Freeman
72 pages $8.00 paper

OTHER LATIN AMERICAN TITLES

STARRY NIGHT
Poems by Marjorie Agosín
Translated by Mary G. Berg
96 pages $12.00

ASHES OF REVOLT
Essays by Marjorie Agosín
128 pages $13.00

REMAKING A LOST HARMONY
Fiction from the Hispanic Caribbean
Translated by Paravisini and Gebert
250 pages $17.00

FALLING THROUGH THE CRACKS
Stories by Julio Ricci
Translated by Clark Zlotchew
82 pages $8.00

HAPPINESS
Stories by Marjorie Agosín
Translated by Elizabeth Horan
238 pages $14.00

CIRCLES OF MADNESS:
MOTHERS OF THE PLAZA DE MAYO
Poems by Marjorie Agosín
Photographs by Alicia D'Amico and Alicia Sanguinetti
Translated by Celeste Kostopulos-Cooperman
128 pages $13.00

MAREMOTO/SEAQUAKE
Poems by Pablo Neruda
Translated by Maria Jacketti & Dennis Maloney
64 pages $9.00   Bilingual

THE STONES OF CHILE
Poems by Pablo Neruda
Translated by Dennis Maloney
98 pages $10.00   Bilingual

SARGASSO
Poems by Marjorie Agosín
Translated by Cola Franzen
92 pages $12.00   Bilingual

LIGHT AND SHADOWS
Poems by Juan Ramon Jimenez
Translated by Robert Bly, Dennis Maloney, Clark Zlotchew
70 pages $9.00

VERTICAL POETRY
Poems by Roberto Juarroz
Translated by Mary Crow
118 pages $11.00   Bilingual

SELECTED POEMS OF MIGUAL HERNANDEZ
Translated by Robert Bly, Timothy Baland, Hardi St Martin and James Wright
138 pages $11.00   Bilingual

About White Pine Press

White Pine Press is a non-profit publishing house dedicated to enriching our literary heritage; promoting cultural awareness, understanding, and respect; and, through literature, addressing social and human rights issues. This mission is accomplished by discovering, producing, and marketing to a diverse circle of readers exceptional works of poetry, fiction, non-fiction, and literature in translation from around the world. Through White Pine Press, authors' voices reach out across cultural, ethnic, and gender boundaries to educate and to entertain.

To insure that these voices are heard as widely as possible, White Pine Press arranges author reading tours and speaking engagements at various colleges, universities, organizations, and bookstores throughout the country. White Pine Press works with colleges and public schools to enrich curricula and promotes discussion in the media. Through these efforts, literature extends beyond the books to make a difference in a rapidly changing world.

As a non-profit organization, White Pine Press depends on support from individuals, foundations, and government agencies to bring you this literature that matters—work that might not be published by profit-driven publishing houses. Our grateful thanks to the many individuals who support this effort as Friends of White Pine Press and to the following organizations: Amter Foundation, Ford Foundation, Korean Culture and Arts Foundation, Lannan Foundation, Lila Wallace-Reader's Digest Fund, Margaret L. Wendt Foundation, Mellon Foundation, National Endowment for the Arts, New York State Council on the Arts, Trubar Foundation, Witter Bynner Foundation, the Slovenian Ministry of Culture, The U.S.-Mexico Fund for Culture, and Wellesley College.

Please support White Pine Press' efforts to present voices that promote cultural awareness and increase understanding and respect among diverse populations of the world. Tax-deductible donations can be made to:

White Pine Press
10 Village Square · Fredonia, NY 14063